Robben,
McKee

Grateful

Peter turned around so his back was to the control panel. He leaned back against the counter, stretching out his sweat-suit-clad legs. He looked up at Monica and grinned. She found his lopsided smile endearing.

"I know we haven't had time to talk much since you've started working here," Peter said. "I just wanted to let you know I'm grateful for your help."

"Oh, it's nothing," Monica said.

"Don't be modest. As a matter of fact, I have a favor to ask. I know Henry left the library a real mess and I was wondering if you wouldn't mind staying after school on Monday to help me sort it out. I'm expecting more records in over the weekend, too, so we'll really have our work cut out for us."

"I wouldn't mind coming in and helping." Monica suprised herself with that offer.

"Great." Peter smiled and walked toward her. "You know, Monica, I think you may be the best thing that ever happened to this radio station."

COUPLES

Books from Scholastic
in the **Couples** series:

MAKING PROMISES

M.E. Cooper

SCHOLASTIC INC.
New York Toronto London Auckland Sydney

ISBN 0-590-33971-0

Copyright © 1986 by Cloverdale Press. All rights re-
served. Published by Scholastic Inc.

12 11 10 9 8 7 6 5 4 3 2 1   1   6 7 8 9/8 0 1/9

Printed in the U.S.A.   06

Chapter
1

Monica Ford stood at the edge of the quad, her eyes scanning the benches scattered between large trees newly green with spring growth. She was looking for Sasha Jenkins, the editor of the Kennedy High paper. Monica was writing an article on the marching band's upcoming trip to Chicago. When Monica spotted Sasha and saw her laughing with her large group of friends, she hesitated. She was sure the crowd would have no interest in hearing about a silly newspaper article, and she had no other reason to join them. Her new friend Kim Barrie, with whom Monica had eaten lunch a couple of times, was not eating lunch today. Kim usually sat with her crowd and her boyfriend, Woody Webster. She had invited Monica to eat with them more than once, but Monica didn't want to be a tag-along.

Monica quickly sat down in an empty seat at a bench filled mostly with freshmen. They were

1

chattering about a quiz one of the English teachers had popped that morning. As Monica eavesdropped, she realized the same teacher had done the same thing in her class two years earlier. Some things never change, she thought, amused.

And some things do, she realized as she took another look at Sasha's bench — like Monica Ford. Resolutely she picked up her tray and walked toward the bench. Unless she took action, she was going to be listening to the same freshman conversations until the end of her senior year.

Monica didn't know where her shyness came from, but ever since kindergarten it had been hard for her to work her way into established friendships, especially with people like Phoebe Hall and Chris Austin. They were the leaders of "The Crowd," as the most visible juniors at Kennedy were known. So Monica had made a special effort to meet Kim when she moved to Rose Hill from Pittsburgh. The two girls had gradually become friends. Monica was especially glad that Kim hadn't seen her as "that quiet girl" she was sophomore year. In fact, when Monica had recently told Kim about her shyness, Kim had scoffed at the idea. She didn't think Monica was shy at all. Kim had also insisted that the other girls were really not as unapproachable as Monica thought. So far, Monica had not tested Kim's assertion. But Sasha had been enthusiastic about her work on the newspaper, and Monica knew Kim was too earthy to be comfortable among snobs.

By the time Monica reached the crowd's

2

bench, the laughter had died, and everyone seemed absorbed in lunch — everyone but Phoebe, whose nose was buried in a New York City guidebook.

Monica tapped Sasha on the shoulder. "Hi, Sasha. Could I talk to you about my article on the band's trip?"

Sasha adjusted the sleeves on her purple gypsy blouse. She patted the seat next to her, where Brad Davidson had been sitting. He'd retreated to a nearby tree to sit with his girl friend, Brenda Austin. "Sure, have a seat," Sasha said. Turning to the table she added, "You all know Monica Ford, don't you?"

"Hi, guys," Monica called out. She gave Chris, who had recently beaten John Marquette in the race for school president, a big smile. "Congratulations, Chris. How does it feel to be student government president?"

"President-elect," Sasha corrected her, with a nod toward Brad, the departing president.

"Sorry," Monica apologized. But Brad seemed too absorbed in Brenda to notice.

Chris beamed. "I never knew so many people at Kennedy knew me. I haven't been able to go anyplace today without someone wishing me well," she admitted. "But I can't say I don't like the feeling."

"Now you know how it feels to score a touchdown," Ted Mason said, rising. "Sorry to break up this lovely gathering, but I've got to get in some cramming before a math quiz." He kissed Chris, and dashed across the quad.

Monica had been listening to the conversation

while Sasha looked over her article, feeling a bit like someone who'd walked in on the third act of a play. She was trying hard to find a way to join the conversation, but so far nothing she'd thought of seemed worth saying aloud.

Just then Woody yanked the New York travel guide out of Phoebe's hands. "You're visiting your boyfriend, not taking a map skills test. You're going to know more about that place than Griffin if you don't watch out."

"That's the idea," she said. "I don't want him thinking I'm some suburban hick going gaga over the big city, which I'll be seeing for the first time. I want him to think I'm really aware of what's going on there."

Monica recalled an article she'd just read in one of her mother's travel magazines, about a hot new Manhattan art gallery. Deciding on the spur of the moment that she had nothing to lose, she cleared her throat and spoke up. "Um, I don't know if this will help, but I've got a suggestion."

"Great," Phoebe cried eagerly. She reached down for her pink canvas bag and picked out a pencil. "I'm open to anything."

"Well, I just read about this new modern art show in SoHo — "

"So *what*?" Phoebe asked.

"It's in lower Manhattan," Woody piped in. He grabbed the book from Phoebe and flipped through the pages. "Here, read all about it."

Phoebe batted her long eyelashes playfully. "Thank you, Mr. Know-It-All." Then to Monica she said seriously, "An art show?"

Monica continued confidently. "The article

4

said it was a 'must see.' I can cut it out and bring it to you tomorrow, if you want."

"That's perfect," Phoebe said. "I like art and I'm sure Griffin does. Thanks, Monica."

"Any time." Kim was right. Phoebe was not unapproachable. Monica had even been able to help her.

Sasha handed Monica back her article on the band. "Not bad, Monica. There are a few changes I'd make — minor ones. Come up to the newspaper office after school and we'll go over it."

"Okay, I — " Monica's response was interrupted by a loud grunt from Brad, who then got up and smacked his hand loudly on his knee.

"Hey, guys, did you hear that?" he called out.

Monica wondered what he meant. All she heard was the usual background clamor, and the music coming from Peter Lacey's radio show on WKND.

"Peter's really blowing it today," Brad continued. "He said he was going to play Culture Club, but up comes Cyndi Lauper. That's the third time it's happened today."

"Maybe he's losing his touch," Woody said.

"More likely it's his assistant's fault," Sasha added. "Last week Peter told me the guy gave away a whole shipment of records. He thought there was something wrong with them, because there weren't any pictures on the covers. Peter had to explain that that's the way they come to radio stations."

As the song ended, Monica heard Peter announce, "Sorry about the mix-up. I think I need to take a refresher course in filing with Ms. Sasso.

Meanwhile, enjoy an oldie-but-goodie from Boy George and friends, 'Do You Really Want to Hurt Me?' "

The group laughed. Ms. Sasso was the business teacher. Once again, Peter had eased out of a mistake. "I have to admit, the guy's smooth," Brad said. "But if I were him I'd can his assistant."

"He'd love to in a minute," Sasha said. "But he can't find anyone to take his place. Organizing records is not exactly a glamour job."

Monica's ears perked up. "Has he really tried?" she asked.

"He's asked around. He'd make an announcement over his show, but he's afraid he'd wind up with a bunch of girls out to make a play for him."

"Sounds egotistical to me," Monica scoffed. "What if a girl were really interested in working with him — to learn about radio, that is?"

"If there was one, I'd have thought he'd have heard from her by now."

"But what if she had no idea her help would be wanted?"

Sasha cocked her head to one side and threw her long, wavy hair off her shoulders. "Why, Monica, are you interested?"

Monica's face began to burn as everyone at the table turned to look at her. Yet she had no trouble speaking her mind. "Yes," she said. "I'm very interested."

Peter Lacey was at the end of his rope. Or rather, he wished he had a rope so he could hang Henry Perkins with it.

Peter slipped his headphones down around his neck. The radio station was like his second home, but ever since Henry had volunteered to help him, it had become more like a madhouse than a sanctuary. At first he had welcomed the sophomore's assistance. Peter had been running the show entirely by himself since Janie Barstow had quit. He had managed all right, although the lack of an extra pair of hands had made the pressure-filled forty-five minute show even more hectic an undertaking.

Peter had been grateful when Henry walked in one afternoon, volunteering his services. Peter hadn't even minded that Henry knew nothing about radio. Janie hadn't either, but she'd had no trouble learning the ropes. Henry, however, turned out to be a first-class loser. He always managed to stack the records in the wrong order, or put them back in the wrong jackets. Peter always had considered himself a patient person, but Henry was pushing him beyond his limits.

The Culture Club record was half over. Peter grabbed another one from the counter, an album by the Jam, and began to set it down on the other turntable. But just as he was about to put the needle down on the record he noticed that it wasn't the Jam, it was the Jangles.

"Henry!" Peter was sure his scream could be heard all over the school, even though his microphone was off.

Henry sauntered into the cramped studio from the record closet. "Yes, boss," he answered innocently.

Peter led him to the turntable. "What does

7

this say?" He pointed to the record.

"The Jangles."

"I asked for the Jam, didn't I?"

Henry looked at Peter, then at the album cover on the counter, and back to Peter. He shrugged helplessly. "Sorry. I must have mixed the two up. I'll go get the record right now."

"I'm coming with you," Peter said, hopping off his stool. He ran his fingers through his short, dark hair, somehow hoping the gesture would help him calm down.

Henry knelt in front of the long shelves that housed the hundreds of records in WKND's library. He quickly began scanning the album spines.

"What in the world are you doing?" Peter's anger was rising with each passing second. "Those are the T's."

"I know," Henry said. "I'm not dumb, Peter, where else would I be looking for The Jam?"

Peter heaved a deep sigh. "I may be dumb myself, but the last time I looked, Jam began with a J."

"But I filed it under T for The," Henry said. "Isn't that the way it's supposed to be done, boss?"

Henry looked up at Peter. He was still squatting, and in that position he reminded Peter a little bit of a frog. They certainly had the same brain size, he thought. "I think you've done enough for today. You can go now, Henry," Peter ordered. "Please," he added plaintively.

The Culture Club record was ending, so Peter quickly grabbed the first record he could from

8

the shelf and threw it on the turntable, just in time to make a smooth transition. He wrinkled his nose in disgust when he heard the first few strains of a Paul Turner record. Peter hated the singer's syrupy voice, but anything was better than dead air.

Peter turned the in-studio monitor down low so he didn't have to hear the music. He wished he could find an assistant who knew what he was doing. None of his friends was willing to give up a lunch period for the thankless task of filing records. And his experience had taught him the worst mistake he could make was to recruit another girl.

His friend Ted liked to say it was the aura of being a DJ that made girls fall at his feet. Sasha said that was nonsense — any girl would find an outgoing guy with drop-dead green eyes, who looked and dressed like a rock star, attractive. At one time she might have fallen for him herself, except she knew she could never love a guy who thought health food was a Hershey bar with almonds.

What his friends thought really didn't make a difference. Peter found the attention more embarrassing than flattering, and went out of his way to avoid flirtatious encounters. But he wasn't sure he could control the situation once he let a girl into the studio. Janie had been working with him for weeks before he had discovered that she had a crush on him.

Then there was Laurie Bennington. Just the thought of her made Peter's stomach turn over. The tall brunette had the face of a Miss America, but she'd never win a Miss Congeniality contest. The latest school rumor was that she'd reformed, but not before hurting a lot of people. She'd talked the student government into allowing her to do an activities report on WKND, as part of her master plan to win Peter. When she failed, she turned her program into a personal gossip session, smearing the reputations of Peter's close friends in spite. Peter had wanted to declare the day she decided to quit the show a national holiday.

There was only one girl Peter would consider as his assistant: his girl friend Lisa. The only problem was that she was two thousand miles away, at a Colorado training center, where she was working on becoming a championship ice skater.

As Peter waited for the record to play out, he reached into his pocket, and reread the last letter she'd written to him. He always carried her letters with him; somehow it helped him feel close to her. He was so proud of her progress these past few months. She'd written to him that she was working on a new routine for the upcoming national team tryouts. She was on the ice six to eight hours a day, and between that and schoolwork she had time to do nothing else. She didn't know when she'd be able to see him again, though she wanted to come back to Rose Hill for a short visit in the summer.

Peter finished reading the letter and shoved it back into the front pocket of his stone-washed Levi's. Summer seemed far away — a lifetime as far as he was concerned. He didn't know how he'd be able to stand the wait.

Chapter
2

"Here, take this rolling pin."

Monica grabbed the long wooden device from Kim's outstretched hand. She began to use it to roll out a ball of dough Kim had placed in the middle of the kitchen table. "Am I doing this right?" she asked Kim.

Kim cast a quick glance at the table as she raced to the refrigerator. "Sure. There's nothing to it." She searched through the rows of containers neatly stacked on the shelves. "Hmmm, Mom said she put the filling in here. Now where is . . . ah, here it is." She took out a large blue plastic tub and set it down on the table. "We've got to hurry. Mom needs these done for a dinner party tonight."

"I'll do whatever you want," Monica said. Kim and her mother ran a catering business, and this wasn't the first time Monica had lent a hand in a pinch. "But I have a favor to ask you, too," she added.

"Anything," Kim said. Using a round serrated cutter she began to stamp out circles in the dough. "You're saving my life by helping me now. It figures Mrs. Fitch would decide to throw a last-minute cocktail party the same night we're catering a shower."

"You're lucky you already have lots of hors d'oeuvres made."

"I hope Mrs. Fitch doesn't notice they were frozen," Kim fretted.

"Don't worry so much. Everything's going to work out just fine. Besides, didn't you tell me Mrs. Fitch was more bark than bite?"

Kim smiled. "You're right. But she's one of our biggest clients now." She let the subject drop, as she began putting spoonfuls of a ground beef mixture in the center of the circles. "I'm sorry, Monica. You said you had something to ask me. What is it?"

Monica gestured toward the books she'd checked out of the public library over the weekend. "I need you to quiz me on those broadcasting books. My meeting with Peter Lacey is tomorrow, after school."

"No problem." Kim smiled. "As soon as we get these into the oven, okay?"

"Sure. That'll be fine."

Kim raised an eyebrow. "Don't tell me you're nervous!"

Monica had picked up the remaining dough and rolled it into a ball in her hands. "I don't want to blow it, Kim. I really want this job."

"I'm sure you'll get it. From what I hear, Peter's pretty desperate."

Monica didn't say anything as she briskly rolled out the rest of the dough. She didn't know if Kim, who plunged into one new activity a week, would understand how much she now wanted to get this job. To her it was more than a gofer's task, it was a stepping-stone to something more meaningful.

Monica hadn't told even Kim yet that she, too, wanted to be a disc jockey. She knew people expected a DJ to be gregarious, lively, and popular — like Peter. She could imagine people's responses when she said that she also wanted to be on the air: What, you? The quiet girl who never has anything to say? But Monica's ambition had come from her shyness, in a way. After a long day at Kennedy High spent taking in all sorts of information without ever really commenting on it, she'd close the door to her room, and take out her cassette recorder. She'd started by recording her version of the Kennedy High news. Then she began to make up introductions to records, the way she'd heard radio disc jockeys do on their own shows.

Monica had thought about working at the Kennedy High radio station for months, but every time she got ready to approach Peter she got cold feet, and backed off. She knew, as did everyone else at Kennedy, that he was very protective of the station. She wasn't sure she could handle being abruptly rejected by him for not meeting his standards. She couldn't quite shake the feeling that the meek Monica Ford still dwelt inside her.

Writing for the newspaper had been a substitute for the radio station, almost. Yet when Monica had heard about Peter's troubles, she knew the opportunity was presenting itself to her. She had actually let Sasha set up the meeting with Peter, and her stomach curled in anxiety just thinking about it.

Kim had finished rolling up the meat pastries and had popped them in the oven. "Okay, I'm ready to help you. What do you want me to do?"

Monica grabbed one of the books and opened it to the first chapter. "Read me the paragraph headings. I'll fill you in."

Kim scanned the page. "The role of broadcasters," she read.

Monica looked up at the off-white ceiling. "The broadcaster has the responsibility to serve the public interest, convenience, and necessity," she began.

Kim put down the book. "Hey, are you sure you've got to know this junk? Peter's not going to give you a test, is he?"

"I don't want him to think I'm an idiot!" Monica said, with a conviction that surprised even her. "These are the kinds of things that all people on the radio have to know about."

"But you're not going to be on the radio. Just helping out."

"Maybe," Monica said, "but I'm sure Peter knows all about the Communications Act of 1934, and emergency broadcast procedures, and the seven forbidden words."

"Ooh, what's that?" Kim wondered.

"Those are the words you're not allowed to say over the air. A station can get its license revoked for that. And that's another thing . . . licensing procedures. I don't even know who owns WKND."

"Peter Lacey, from what I understand. I don't mean literally — the school board must, or something."

"But you see what I mean? Peter is passionate about that station. He treats it like his own baby. I want to show him that as his assistant, I'll have that same kind of passion and devotion."

Kim looked at her friend curiously. "Why the concern about what he thinks?"

"I really want this," Monica admitted. "I may want to get into broadcasting someday, and this is the closest I can come right now."

"Then go for it. I know what it means to really want something. Look how hard I work with my mom on this business." She picked up the book. "Now let me see where I was." She flipped through the book, and placed a neatly trimmed fingernail on the center of a page. "Ah, equal time rules. . . ."

Monica didn't get a chance to answer as Kim was interrupted by a knock on the back door. She skipped past the mud room, and let in Woody. Her boyfriend was carrying a large paper bag from the sub shop.

"Greetings, ladies. I thought you might be hungry, so I brought a couple of salami and turkey subs," he said.

Kim smirked, and gave Woody a playful punch

in the ribs. "Woodrow, darling, your offer is much appreciated. But what do my mother and I do for a living?"

"Run a catering service."

"What's the one thing in the world we never run out of in this house?"

"Food?" he asked, getting the drift of her message.

Monica saw Woody's face fall. "I'll take mine," she said. "Making all these meat pastries made me hungry."

"A girl after my own heart," Woody said, patting her affectionately on the shoulder. "Salami or turkey?" he asked, unwrapping the sandwiches.

"Salami. But just half," she added. "I'm not that hungry."

Woody began to talk as he took a plate out of the cabinet. "I ran into Brad and Brenda at the sub shop. They told me Ted's throwing a surprise party to celebrate Chris's election."

"Sounds like fun. When is it?" Kim asked. Woody grinned at her as she reached for half of the turkey sub.

"Saturday night. At Phoebe's. But remember it's a surprise. Don't tell a soul. I'm surprised they told me. You know I can't keep a secret."

"Don't worry, Woody. I'll watch you like a hawk," Kim said.

Monica was concentrating on her sandwich, trying hard to ignore her friends' conversation. She thought it was nice of Ted to throw a party for his girl friend. But she really didn't want to hear all the details about a party she wouldn't be attending.

"Hey, Monica, why the long face?" Kim broke into her thoughts. "Are you busy Saturday night?"

"But I wasn't invited to the party."

"Are you deaf?" Woody asked. "Didn't I just come in here and tell you about it? This is *not* the kind of affair that calls for engraved invitations."

"I don't have a date."

"So what?" Now Woody was laughing. "Our parties are never for couples only. Gosh, if they were I'd have been a social outcast before Kim came along. You're coming to this party, Monica Ford. That's an order. Got it?" He paused as he sniffed the air. "Hey, what's that I smell?"

"The pastries!" both girls cried out at the same time.

Chapter
3

Monica thought everything would work out fine — as long as she remembered to smile.

She was checking herself in the bathroom mirror one last time, her meeting with Peter just minutes away. Her shoulder-length dark blond hair was parted on the side. She had on enough pink lipstick and blush to give her face some color, but not look like it had too much makeup. A pastel yellow sweater and royal-blue skirt were casual enough to pass for regular school wear, but also fresh enough to make a good impression.

But something wasn't right. Monica checked her face again, and there it was. Her nervousness was written all over her face. Her teeth were so tightly clenched together that they gave her face a hard, almost challenging look. Was that how she appeared to the outside world, when inside she was full of butterflies? She forced herself to smile.

Checking her watch, Monica realized she had to leave if she was to keep her appointment with Peter. She grabbed her books and shoulder bag, and marched down the hall to the radio station.

The door was partly open so Monica knocked gently, then walked in. She was surprised. It was a lot smaller than she'd imagined, and a whole lot messier. Records were stashed all over the counter next to the control board, along with a couple of notepads, some empty soda cans, and candy wrappers. Clearly Peter needed a helping hand. But he was not in sight.

Monica could feel the worry returning to her face. Maybe she had the wrong day. Maybe Peter forgot about their appointment. As she considered the possibilities with mounting distress, she spotted another door to a room that had a light on. She ventured closer.

It was then that Peter saw her. He moved out of the record closet, closing the door behind him. "Oh, hi," he said. "Let's talk. I've got a lot of records to put away." He sounded stiff, much more formal than his casual radio voice. "I go through plenty during my show."

"I know," Monica said. "You played twelve today."

Peter snorted. "You actually counted?"

Monica tried to make light of it. "I wanted to see how many records I'd have to keep track of, if I became your assistant."

Peter looked her straight in the eye. "Let me give it to you straight. Uh, I'm sorry, what's your name?"

"Monica. Monica Ford." She felt her face

redden. Why was she feeling embarrassed, she wondered, when he was the one who couldn't remember her name?

"Monica," he repeated. "I told Sasha I'd see you as a favor to her. But the truth is, I'm not looking for another assistant."

Monica froze. She knew he was lying, but didn't know why. Her first inclination was to blame herself, but she quickly wiped the thought from her mind. The new Monica didn't think that way anymore. The new Monica didn't think was trying to test her. She walked to the microphone hanging over the control panel on a swinging arm. "Is that bi-directional or uni-directional?"

Peter smirked. "You know about that stuff?"

"It makes all the difference in the world. With the wrong type of microphone you can sound as if you're broadcasting out of a garbage can."

"That's true," he said, shaking his head. No other girl at Kennedy had ever let on she knew there were different kinds of microphones, let alone cared about it. Even Janie had never asked him about his equipment. "Do you know what that black thing covering the mike is?"

"Sure, a windscreen. It helps make your voice sound better. I didn't think you needed one." Monica's eyes wandered around the tiny studio. "Where are the cart machines?" she asked.

"What you see is what you get." Peter held out his arms. "Just the basics here — two turntables and a microphone."

"I was wondering why you never do sound effects, or play excerpts from sixties TV shows, like the stations in D.C. do."

"You seem to know a lot about equipment," Peter said. "Let's talk about the record library. Do you know how to file?"

"Well, sure," Monica said, somewhat confused by Peter's sudden enthusiasm. "I've worked as a file clerk in my mother's real estate office on vacations."

"Great. You're hired," he said. For the first time since Monica's arrival Peter smiled, revealing a gleaming set of white teeth, and just the hint of two dimples in his chin.

Emboldened by the success of her approach, Monica questioned him. "I thought you said you didn't need help."

Peter pressed his lips together in a smirk. "I should have known Sasha would send me someone smart enough to know when I was lying. Can I be honest with you, Monica?" He leaned against the counter.

"Now's as good a time as any to start." She folded her arms, and chuckled to herself. She enjoyed the strange feeling that *she* was now in control of this interview.

"Two points." He licked his finger and drew two imaginary lines in the air between them. "You seem like a nice girl, Monica. And since the job's yours, you might as well know about this. I need an assistant badly; the guy who's helping now is a real mess. But I didn't want to take on a girl. I've had some bad experiences with girls misunderstanding my working hard, or spending a lot of time at the station. But I'd be a huge egomaniac if I thought that was why you came here. I think it's really the station that

21

matters to you." He paused. "Is something the matter?"

Monica realized she'd stopped smiling. "Is that it? That's all it takes to get this job? I stayed up all night, reading half a dozen books about radio. Would you like to hear me recite all the rules and regulations in the Communications Act?"

Peter slapped his hand on his knee and started to laugh. "That's great, Monica. I don't believe it." He continued to chuckle.

"I don't see what's so funny," she said under her breath.

"I'm sorry," Peter said, regaining control of himself. "I wasn't laughing at you, really. See, I did the same thing myself. Do you know Mr. Leibenhaven? If you don't now, you will soon. He's the station's faculty advisor. The night before my interview with him I memorized this article I'd read called 'The Ten Golden Rules of the Media.' He never asked me anything about it. All he wanted to know was if I knew how to run this board. I said yes. He said, 'You've got a show.' And the rest is history."

"Oh."

"Please don't be mad with me. I'm glad you're interested in the equipment. Do you know how to run a board, too?"

"No, but I'd like to learn."

"Maybe I'll teach you one of these days," he said, flashing another smile.

"I'd like that," she said. She darted her eyes away from Peter and toward the compact control panel. Right above it she noticed an album by Pirate Cove. "I've never heard you play this on your show," she told him, lifting up the record. "I wish you would. It's one of my favorites."

"Mine, too," he said. "I was listening to it just before you came. How do you know I've never played it?"

"I'm a very devout listener."

"Then you know I play mostly hits. I don't think Rose Hill is ready for Pirate Cove. They're pretty funky. Whenever I've tried to play the stuff I like, I've gotten lots of complaints."

"But what about requests? Suppose someone started calling up and demanding you play this record? What would you do then?"

"I never turn down requests."

"Then maybe I'll start calling in."

"But you'll be working here with me."

Monica shrugged. "So I'll sneak out to the pay phone when you're not looking." Monica couldn't believe how easy it was to talk with Peter. With the radio station to talk about, she didn't have to worry about what to say next. And Peter had made it clear that he had only business on his mind. Monica almost laughed, thinking about the knots she had tied herself in all morning long.

"As long as you don't leave me with the Jangles instead of the Jam, it's fine with me."

"Huh?"

Peter shook his head. "Never mind."

"So when do you want me to start?"

"Tomorrow."

"So soon?"

"Is it a problem? Do you want to have a final lunch with your friends, or something?"

"No," Monica said. She wasn't going to miss

eating with the rest of the school. She was about to start something a whole lot more appealing. "I'll see you tomorrow at noon."

"Great." Peter got up and showed her to the door. "I'll be looking forward to it. I think you're going to work out just fine."

Chapter
4

"Hey, guys, you really didn't have to come out here with me." Sasha looked gratefully at Chris, Phoebe, and Woody, who were sitting next to her on the grass adjacent to the athletic fields. A girls' soccer game was in progress.

"Nonsense," Chris said. "We know you know absolutely nothing about soccer. I'm surprised you're doing this in the first place."

"I told you, the flu bug's got all the usual sports reporters. And Andy McKinney, the sports editor, is covering a tennis match."

"I'd just as soon be here as anyplace else," Phoebe added, her head buried in a map of New York City.

"Me, too," piped up Woody. "Kim's gone shopping with her mother, and didn't want me tagging along. Besides, I think I'll like spending the afternoon watching all these girls run around in shorts."

"Sexist." Sasha bopped him on the head with her notepad. Turning to Phoebe she asked, "Got New York figured out yet?"

Phoebe nodded. "I think so. All the avenues run north-south, and all the streets run east-west. Or is it the other way around?" Biting her lower lip, she double-checked the map.

"You know, Pheeb," Woody said, "I've been thinking. I'm not sure it is a good idea for you to go to New York alone — I mean with just my mom." He pulled at the tufts of grass beneath his right hand. "Maybe you should wait until someone who already knows avenues from streets can go, too."

Phoebe laughed. Woody was just about the best friend who happened to be a boy she had. Now that he was dating Kim their friendship had, ironically, become better than ever. She felt more comfortable talking with him about her romantic problems, such as her upcoming trip to visit her boyfriend, Griffin.

It had always bothered her when Woody wanted something more out of their relationship than she could possibly give him. But as much as she tried, she just couldn't imagine even kissing him. It would be like kissing her younger brother, Shawn. She'd been delighted when Woody found Kim, whose infectious spirit and assertiveness were perfectly suited to Woody.

Woody had helped Phoebe hatch the plan that would enable her to see Griffin. Knowing that her overprotective parents would never allow her to travel to New York by herself, she'd had to devise a way to get there that would alleviate their

26

worries, yet still enable her to see Griffin. Woody had stumbled on the answer when he'd mentioned that his mother, a local theater administrator, was planning a weekend trip to New York to meet with some theater directors. The hardest part was convincing her parents. But they gave their nods of approval when Woody's mother agreed to take Phoebe along, and let her stay in her hotel suite.

"Don't be a dope, Woody. This whole thing was your plan. Yesterday you told me I'd be just fine. And I will, as long as I read my guide-books."

"I don't know, Pheeb. I'm not sure you should have such confidence in one of my harebrained schemes. Anyway, it rains a lot in New York this time of year. Maybe you should wait until fall."

"Woody, stop it. You couldn't keep me from getting to Griffin now, no matter what you said."

"Where does Griffin live?" Sasha asked.

"On someplace called Great Jones Street. I'm still trying to find it. Contrary to what Woody has told me, not all the streets have numbers."

"But if it's a street it must run east-west, right?" Sasha insisted.

Phoebe stuck her finger on the map. "Here it is. It's kind of on an angle," She threw the map down on the grass. "Gosh, how am I ever going to learn all this by next week?"

Chris turned her eyes from the game and faced Phoebe. "I still don't see why you're going to all this trouble. Why don't you just tell Griffin the truth, that you've never been to New York? I'll bet he'd love to show you around."

"Like I'm a dumb tourist? No way," Phoebe declared. A slight breeze blew wisps of her red hair into her eyes. Using her fingers as a comb, she brushed them back across her forehead. "Look at it from my perspective. Griffin's been studying acting in New York for months, and has been exposed to a lot of sophisticated actresses. I don't want him to take one look at me, see I don't know anything about the city, and decide he's wasted all this time waiting for me. I really want to impress him."

"Sounds fishy to me," Chris scoffed. "I'd love to have a guy give me a guided tour of the city."

"I fully intend to let Griffin do that. But when we do, I want to be able to point out things I know about, too. I was reading about this old church downtown that someone turned into a disco."

"Maybe he'll take you there," Chris said.

"I don't know if we'll be able to get in," Phoebe said. "Or whether we'll even have time. Griffin's doing a play at his acting school, and I think afterward he's going to want to introduce me to his teacher. Griffin says this man's been like a father to him, and he has really helped him become a better actor. I can't wait to see what he's talking about. I thought he was pretty good before he left here."

Just then there was a commotion on the field. "Hey, did anyone see what happend?" Sasha asked, panicking. She took her reporting work seriously, even though she was finding Phoebe's situation far more interesting.

Chris pointed to the far side of the field, where

several red-shirted girls were patting the shoulder of another player. "Our team just scored a goal, or actually, that girl did." She squinted her blue eyes to get a better look. "Oh, I know her. That's Sally Palmieri. She's in student government."

Sasha was furiously writing all this down. At the same time she said, "If it's a nice day you should try to spend some time in Central Park — have a picnic, or something. It could be very romantic."

Phoebe wrinkled her nose. "People really walk there? Isn't it full of muggers?"

"Not in the middle of the afternoon. When I was up there last summer visiting my cousin Rachel, I saw lots of couples walking around. You could go bike riding or rowing. It's really kind of neat."

Phoebe added this to her growing list. "I'll think about it. You know, I never found out if Griffin's a sports fan. I read that the Yankees are going to be there next weekend. I'd like to see them play."

Woody gulped and looked as green as if he'd just swallowed a handful of dirt. He scootched back a little from Phoebe. "Uh, Phoebe. . . ." he began tentatively.

Immediately, she sensed something was wrong. Woody hardly ever called her Phoebe, preferring his elongated pet name for her. "What's wrong, Woody?" she demanded.

"It's about the weekend," he said.

"What about it? Your mother's not going?"

"She's going. And you're welcome to go along. But there's been a slight change."

"Woody, you've already made me miserable. So you might as well spit it out."

"My mother's meeting was pushed back to the middle of the following week."

"Middle? As in not on the weekend?"

Woody nodded his head. "She says you're still welcome to stay with her."

"Woody, how could I? What am I going to do now? You know all the trouble I had to go through to get Mom and Dad to agree to let me go with her."

"Maybe they still will," he said.

"My parents? The modern-day equivalents of medieval gatekeepers? The only reason I got them to agree to let me go in the first place, was because I was able to successfully shoot down every single argument they raised. There's no way on earth they're going to let me miss two days of school."

"Would you consider a small deception?"

"No! The last time I tried that I got grounded for a month." She started to raise a finger to her mouth, ready to bite off a nail in frustration, but she thought better of it. What good would it do her to have a messed-up plan *and* messed-up fingernails? She kicked up a clod of grass instead. It's just not fair! she cried to herself. For once, her rocky relationship with Griffin had been sailing smoothly. But every time they tried to get together, something eventually came up to thwart their plans. Phoebe didn't know what she was going to do, but she was going to find a way around this latest roadblock.

Chapter
5

"This is Monica Ford, bringing you all the hits on WKND."

Monica giggled to herself, as she leaned back from the WKND microphone Friday afternoon. This is really fun, she thought, as she looked at the albums cued up and ready for play on the station's two turntables. All I have to do is flip that switch. . . .

She gave a long look to the red toggle switch on the far end of the master control board. If she pushed it to the right she would turn on the staion transmitter, and be heard all over the campus. She knew she wouldn't. It had taken all the nerve she could muster, just to sneak out of study hall fifteen minutes early to get to the station before Peter arrived. She wanted to surprise him, and show him that she cared as much about the station as he did.

Monica looked around the cramped, airless

room, and had to stifle another giggle. Paradise. She loved every square inch of the place, from the Talking Heads poster on the wall over the turntables, and the chipped acoustical tile in the ceiling, to the green carpet that had been tromped on too many times. She knew it was absurd; anyone else looking at the room would think it was a dump. But she knew she felt things other people wouldn't, like the excitement of seeing the red ON THE AIR light go on, and sensing the power of being able to reach out and communicate with anyone in Rose Hill; and the feeling that, as insignificant as her job might be, she was working at a real live radio station.

The sound of footsteps made her turn around suddenly. There was Peter striding purposefully through the station door, the latest issue of *Rolling Stone* tucked under his arm. Quickly, she jumped off the stool he sat on during his programs. But he didn't look unhappy to see her there.

"I can't believe you got here first," he said, his eyes twinkling over his dimpled smile. "What did you do, fly?"

"No, I took the more conventional route — I cut part of study hall," she told him. "I read over that manual you lent me yesterday, and came early to practice cueing up records." She pointed to the turntables.

Peter moved over and studied the labels. "Hmm, you've got good taste. Do you mind if I start off my show with these?"

Monica looked at him, wide-eyed. As far as she was concerned that was as a big a compliment as the time Mr. Satin read her English essay in front of the class.

Peter winked playfully. "Hey, don't answer at once." Quickly moving around Monica, he put his magazine on the counter and looked up at the clock. It was two minutes to twelve. Flipping through the magazine he took out a single sheet of paper, and handed it to Monica. "Here, find me these tunes," he ordered, his voice sounding more businesslike.

It didn't take her long to find the first album on the list. She carried it into the studio just ten seconds before he was ready to go on the air. She still couldn't believe Peter wanted to go with the records she selected. He managed to give her a thumbs-up sign as she closed the door behind her. Looking up, she noticed the ON THE AIR light was on.

Returning to the closet, Monica turned up the speaker control next to the door and listened to the program. Peter was finishing the introduction to the record she'd set up for him.

Then Monica winced. The record made a "wowwing" sound as Peter turned up the volume. She hadn't cued the record properly. She dreaded hearing what Peter would have to say about that. In the two days she'd worked with him she had found him to be so totally dedicated to the show, that she doubted he would be tolerant of her mistake. Monica wanted to kick herself. She had hoped to impress him.

To try to make amends, she quickly picked out the rest of the records on the list. At least she knew how to do that right.

Before going back to the studio Monica stopped to watch Peter work. He was talking about the groups who would be touring the Washington area in the next few weeks. Monica was careful not to make any noise. Even though the closed studio door was between Peter and her, she didn't want to take any chances on ruining his concentration.

It was silly, she realized. It would be hard to distract Peter, even if the door was open. She'd never seen anyone as focused on anything as Peter was while he was on the air. He was always on top of things, never letting even a second escape that wasn't filled with music, or the sound of his voice. She loved the way he got into the music, too, bouncing up and down on his stool or, every once in a while, even getting up and dancing on the tiny patch of green carpet.

After she dropped off the records in the studio, Monica went back to the record library. She'd already put away the records from the previous day's show and was now scanning the shelves to familiarize herself with the entire collection. Still in the A's, she spotted one by Amos Allright. She'd never heard of him, and took it out to see if she could learn something from the album's liner notes.

She was still reading it when there was a knock on the open door. "Say, Monica, I just got a request. Could you get me 'Crazy in the Night' by — "

"Eddie Ross. Coming right up," she answered.

Peter winked at her. "It's great to have someone around who knows what she's doing."

Monica smiled, but she still felt bad about her earlier goof. "I'm sorry I messed up your first record."

"Oh, that," Peter scoffed. "No big deal. I was happy you were here early enough to have something ready for me to play. Mrs. Carson didn't hand back our tests until after the bell rang, and I thought I'd have to go on late today. Thanks to you I didn't. I can forgive a little wowwing for that." Just then he noticed the album in her hand. "One of the best reggae artists in the world. You like him?"

Monica shrugged. "I've never heard him."

"We're not allowed to take records out of here, but you're welcome to come by after school any day and play it, or anything else around here. I'm usually around."

"I'll keep that in mind," Monica said.

Peter went back to the studio. Monica refiled the reggae record and began to look for Eddie Ross, but she couldn't find it. Feeling nervous, she went back and forth over the R's half a dozen times, just to make sure. But it wasn't there. Maybe it wasn't around anymore? She quickly shook that notion from her head. Peter surely knew by heart every single record in the library.

Then Monica remembered what Peter had told her about Henry's strange filing system. She searched through the E's. Still no album.

Feeling defeated, she slunk into the studio. "Excuse me, Peter, but I can't find it." The apology was thick in her voice. She felt as if she were really letting him down.

"I know it's here. I played a cut from it two weeks ago. Did you check the E's?" he asked.

"Yes," Monica said.

Peter looked surprised. "Hmm, I thought that'd do it." Then he snapped his fingers. "Check C for Crazy."

Monica smiled. "Be right back."

Less than a minute later she returned with the album. "I don't think I'll ever understand how Henry did things."

"I don't want you to," Peter said. "I'd hate to see you pick up his bad habits." He twisted over to the turntable, but motioned for her to stay.

Monica watched carefully as he slowly turned down the level on the first record, while gently raising the level of Eddie Ross. The transition between the two songs was so seamless that if she hadn't known better, she would have thought it was one continuous piece of music.

Peter turned around so his back was to the control panel. He leaned back against the counter, stretching out his sweat-suit-clad legs. He looked up at Monica and grinned. She found his lopsided smile endearing.

"I know we haven't had time to talk much since you've started working here," Peter said. "I just wanted to let you know I'm grateful for your help."

"Oh, it's nothing," Monica said.

"Don't be modest. Since you've been here I haven't made any screw-ups over the air. That means an awful lot to me."

Monica was sure her face was blushing as red as a stoplight. She lowered her head so Peter wouldn't notice, and began to back out of the room.

But he wasn't through. "Wait a second, Monica. I sort of have a favor to ask. I know Henry left the library a real mess, and I was wondering if you wouldn't mind staying after school on Monday to help me sort it out. I'm expecting more records in over the weekend, too, so we'll have our work cut out for us."

"I wouldn't mind staying late on Monday and helping." Monica surprised herself with that offer.

Peter shook his head. "I'll see you here, then."

"You bet," she said.

"Great." Peter smiled, and walked toward her. "You know, Monica, I think you may be the best thing that ever happened to this radio station.

"I see you've got a new assistant," an unfamiliar voice interrupted.

Monica could see Peter's smile turn flat as a pancake as Laurie Bennington marched into the studio. She hadn't bothered to knock.

"What's it to you, Bennington? Are you heartbroken I didn't ask you first?"

Monica did a double take. This boy didn't sound like the Peter she'd worked with all week. Then she quickly remembered — for a while, Laurie had broadcast a student government activities report on Peter's show. The way Peter had introduced her made it clear he didn't care for her. It was a feeling that a large part of the student body shared. In the year she had been at Kennedy, Laurie had earned the reputation of someone who would not be content until she had the entire school under her control. Monica was always surprised to hear about this beautiful, intelligent girl's latest scheme to increase her own popularity. The latest news was that she had been transformed by her new relationship with Dick Westergard. But Monica sensed that the people Laurie had used in the past weren't quite ready to trust her.

Laurie rested her arm on Peter's shoulder and replied sweetly, "I'm afraid I'd have to turn you down, Peter. I'm too busy. But I'm sure I'd have liked it."

"Don't flatter yourself, Laurie," he said, slipping away from her grasp. "If you were the last person left in this school, I wouldn't have asked you."

"Oh, Peter, don't tell me you're still mad at me."

"And why not? You made a joke of this radio station with your poor excuse for an activities program."

"That was eons ago, Peter," Laurie said. "And you may not believe this, but I think you're right."

Peter nodded. "You're right. I don't believe you."

Laurie lowered her eyelids. They were layered with more eyeshadow than Monica had used in the past year. "I owe you a big apology for the way I used to behave. But I've grown up a lot since then; I'm not like that anymore."

Peter's sneer softened, yet the slight squint of his eyes betrayed his skepticism of Laurie's apology. Monica almost felt sorry for Laurie. It was going to take a lot more work to earn a good reputation than it had to earn a bad one. Peter continued, "What am I supposed to do? Give you a medal?"

"I don't want you to do anything, Peter," she said, her voice returning to a more normal tone. She drifted over to the turntables, and ran a pink manicured nail over one of the tone arms. "I came here to tell you about something Dick and I talked about last night. Now that he's going to be vice-president next year, he's thinking of reviving the activities program."

Peter's face began to redden with anger. "I'll go to the school board if I have to, but there's no way you're ever going back on the air here."

"I don't want to, Peter," she said.

"You don't? Then, what — "

"Give me a chance to speak and maybe you'll find out. Dick wasn't thrilled with my old show, either. But he really believes we need a student government voice on the air. He plans to bring it up for consideration at the next student government meeting. I just came here to give you advance notice. If you want to object to the idea, that's the place to do it."

"Maybe I'll do that," Peter said, clearly confused by Laurie's message.

"I know you'll do the right thing," she said. "I've got to run now. See you around." Turning on her heel she pranced out the door just as quickly as she had come in.

"What was that all about?" Peter said aloud.

Monica, who'd watched the exchange with mounting interest, shook her head. "Beats me.

I've never met Laurie before, but she seemed more like a pussycat than the tiger I've heard about."

"I don't trust her," Peter said. "Tigers don't change their stripes overnight. Laurie Bennington can't be trusted." Peter began stacking records. His earlier relaxed mood had disappeared.

Monica sighed. She'd never seen Laurie in action before, so she didn't know if Peter was right. But she was sure of one thing — Laurie Bennington had a really bad sense of timing.

Chapter 6

"Chris, this is Phoebe. I've got to talk with you!"

Chris was upset by the distress in her friend's voice. "My gosh, Phoebe, what's wrong?"

"My life is a mess," Phoebe admitted. "How in the world am I going to get to New York?"

"Did your parents say no?"

Phoebe sighed. "I haven't had the guts to ask them yet, Chris. Every time I think about it, I hear them saying. 'Well, Phoebe, no sane parents would let their daughter cut school to visit her boyfriend.' That's why I'm calling. I need your help. Could you come over and give me moral support?"

Chris bit her lip. She wanted to do what she could to help Phoebe get together with Griffin, especially after the way she'd acted at the beginning of their relationship. Phoebe had been dating Brad at the time, and Chris had not liked the idea of their breaking up. So instead of acting like a friend, Chris had acted like Phoebe's mother, lecturing her instead of giving her encouragement. It had nearly caused the end of their friendship, and Chris had vowed never to let Phoebe down again. But Ted was going to be at her front door in ten minutes. It was too late to reach him. "I can come first thing in the morning," she told Phoebe.

Phoebe pressed on. "Believe me, Chris, I'd never ask you to do this if it weren't important. Could you come over right now?"

Chris looked at her watch. "Ted'll be picking me up any minute."

"Bring him along," Phoebe said.

"Are you kidding? Ted's not much help when it comes to romance. He'll make fun of you."

"He can stay in the car. It'll just take a few minutes," Phoebe pleaded. "I won't ruin your date. I promise."

Chris thought quickly. "All right. I hope Ted doesn't mind. He said he was looking forward to a nice, relaxing evening. See you in a few minutes."

Phoebe had to try hard to suppress a laugh as she hung up the phone. She knew Ted wouldn't mind in the least. After all, not only had it been his idea in the first place, he was standing right next to her when she made the call. "It's all set," she told him. "And Chris doesn't suspect a thing."

Monica struggled to fasten the buttons on her dress with the tiny puff sleeves. "What do you think?" she asked Kim, as she finished.

Kim rested her chin on her fists. "I think you're overdressed," she announced. She was wearing a white and peach striped sweater over a pair of jeans and ankle-high boots.

Monica threw up her hands in frustration. "I don't have anything to wear!" she cried.

Kim got up from Monica's bed, and walked over to a pair of pants discarded earlier. "Listen to me, and wear your red sweater with these," she said. "I don't know why you're driving yourself crazy. It's only an informal party."

"I know. But it's the first time I've ever been to Phoebe's house. I don't want to stick out like a sore thumb."

"Then don't wear that dress," Kim implored. "Here." She handed Monica the pants. "Woody'll be picking us up soon."

"But I've still got to put on my makeup!"

Kim shook her head. "Hey, lighten up, will you?"

Monica grimaced as she got undressed. "You're right. Sorry."

"Come on, Monica, what's up? I've never seen you so nervous about a party. And don't give me that line about Phoebe. You know her well enough to realize she's one of the most unpretentious people in the world."

"You're right. It's not Phoebe." She walked over to her dresser and pulled out the red angora sweater her mother had given her for Christmas. "It's a boy."

Monica had been unable to get Peter out of her thoughts since she'd last seen him. As mindful as she was of his warnings about turning her work with him at the station into anything else, she was sure he had been feeling the same attraction she did on Friday. She also felt a need to test her feelings about him, to see how much of what attracted her to the station had to do with the work, and how much had to do with Peter.

She had been a little worried that she hadn't heard him talk about the party all week. She'd been planning to ask him about it, when Laurie Bennington had arrived and aggravated him so that Monica felt she couldn't approach him. But she was certain he would be at the party. Chris Austin was one of his closest friends.

Kim smacked her forehead. "I should have known. Are you going to tell me who it is, or do I have to play twenty questions?"

"I'm not ready to tell you," Monica said, entering the small blue bathroom off her bedroom. "I don't want to feel like a fool if he's not interested in me. I'm not even sure he's going to be there tonight. But if he is, you'll find out soon enough."

"You're going to an awful lot of trouble for someone who might be a no-show." Kim followed Monica into the bathroom, and leaned against the shower door.

"My girl scout leader told me to always be prepared." Monica held her right hand over her left eyelid and took a deep breath. This was one night she was going to have perfectly straight lines on the edge of her eyelids.

"Well, I hope it works out for you," Kim said.

Monica didn't say a word until she finished

what was, for her, an arduous task. But it was worth it. The soft gray lines made her hazel eyes look darker and along with her dark blond hair gave her a more mysterious appearance, which was exactly what she wanted. "You can understand, can't you, Kim?" she asked. "I mean, you've got Woody, Chris has Ted, Brenda has Brad, and Phoebe has Griffin. I've never had a one-on-one relationship like that. I've been on dates, I even dated someone for a couple of months — but nothing really serious, or meaningful."

"I wish everybody could have just half of what Woody and I do," Kim said. "I'd do anything to help you, too. But I can't, if you won't tell me who he is."

"Not yet," Monica repeated. "But when I'm ready, you'll be the first to know."

Monica crouched behind the baby grand in the Halls' living room with Kim and Woody. Each time the collected group heard a car in the driveway, they ran for cover, while Phoebe checked for Chris's arrival. Monica was torn between the anticipation of the surprise and her hope for Peter's arrival. So far, he hadn't turned up, and no one had mentioned his absence.

"It's them," Phoebe hissed as she dropped the curtain behind the living room window.

As the couple got closer, Monica could hear their voices. "I'll keep Shawn occupied if I have to," Ted said. "You two girls can take all the time you need to talk."

"I wonder if Phoebe's parents are even home," Chris said. "The place looks pretty dark."

"No one ever uses the living room. They're probably in the den watching TV." Monica heard Phoebe giggle.

Chris rang the doorbell. Phoebe opened the door before the chime had rung through its four-bell greeting.

"Hello, sucker!" Phoebe cried. Just then she flipped on the lights and everyone emerged to shout, "Surprise!"

Chris covered her face with her hands. "I don't believe this!" she cried. Then she turned to Ted. "You knew all about this, didn't you?"

"It was my idea." He kissed her on the cheek. "Congratulations, Madam President."

Chris looked as if she were going to cry as she surveyed the room Phoebe, Ted, and Woody had set up that afternoon. Multicolored balloons filled the entire room, and draped across the fireplace mantel was a huge banner that read, HAIL TO THE NEW CHIEF — CHRIS. Every partygoer wore a button that read: Chris is #1. The surprise on Chris's face revealed that she had not had any notion this party was going to take place.

Chris's stepsister Brenda threw her arms around her. "Come on in and join the party."

Chris shook her head. "You knew about this, too? I thought you and Brad were going into Georgetown."

"We did. To pick up your present. Come on over here, we'll open it."

"Presents, too? Listen, guys, you've done

enough for me already. You didn't have to get me anything."

"Don't get all wound up. It's just a gag gift," said Brenda.

"Oh, Brenda, I don't care what it is." Impulsively Chris threw her arms around her stepsister. "I'm so glad you're here."

Brenda pushed her back. "Hey, no waterworks tonight, okay? We're all here to have a good time. Let's party."

Phoebe had already turned up the volume on the stereo, and everyone was getting into a party spirit. Sasha had pushed the coffee table and a couple of chairs against the wall to open up room for dancing. She started to move around by herself, but was soon joined by Jamie McMichael, one of the guys in her government class. Janie Barstow and Henry Braverman soon followed.

"Now, that's getting the party off to a good start," Woody said, as he walked toward Kim and Monica with a cola in his hand. The three of them stood near the fireplace, passing the can of soda back and forth.

"Let's join them," Kim urged.

"These feet were made for dancing," Woody said, grinning. "But first let me get something more to eat."

"Can you believe I put up with this?" Kim complained to Monica as Woody made his way to the food.

Monica smiled. "I could think of worse ways to spend a night."

"That's right, you actually laugh at Woody's

cornball jokes. By the way, has your mystery guy shown up yet?"

"Not yet." Monica kept her eyes turned to the front door, looking for Peter. A few late arrivals had walked in since Chris had come, so she felt it was too early to give up hope.

"I see Chris is getting ready to open her presents," Kim said.

They wandered over to the dining area. Chris was standing next to the table with several boxes in front of her. "I feel like it's my birthday," she said, picking up a box. She shook it to hear what was inside.

"It's from Brad and me," Brenda said proudly.

"Then I'll definitely open it up first." Chris tore off the blue sash and opened up the rectangular box. Inside was a gavel, made out of chocolate. "It's great," Chris said. "Thanks a lot."

"We had it specially made by this place in Georgetown. Go on, eat it."

"It looks too good to eat," Chris said. "I'm going to put it on the shelf in my room."

"And watch it get all gross and stale? Yecch," Brenda chided her.

Chris agreed it would be ridiculous to let the chocolate go to waste. She broke off the top of the handle and gave it to Brenda. "You get the first bite." She reached for the next box and opened it. She took out what looked like a macrame basket, with several straps attached. The card inside the box read FROM SASHA. "It's lovely," she said diplomatically. "But what is it?"

Sasha threw back her long, wavy hair and giggled. "It's a muzzle. To be used to keep Laurie

Bennington and other troublemakers quiet during student government meetings."

"Great. I'll definitely need this," she said as she began unwrapping a third present. The small box was empty, except for the words *Love, Phoebe and Woody* scrawled on the bottom. Chris looked puzzled. "I don't get it."

"That's our cue, Woody." Phoebe led him to the piano in the living room. Woody sat down and began to play the Kennedy school song. But instead of the usual words, Phoebe sang:

Hail to thee, our dear Chris Austin,
New school president.
She's so smart and always punctual,
A fine Rose Hill resident.

She believes in following rules,
Like always to class on time.
She does her homework and gets all A's,
But for some reason we like her fine.

Soon she'll lead us all together,
As leader of our high.
But if you cross her, heaven forgive you,
She'll have Ted give you a black eye.

Phoebe made an exaggerated bow as a chorus of boos and applause greeted the end of her song.

Chris had backed herself into a corner. "I don't believe this!" she cried. "That's the worst song I ever heard."

"Thanks," Woody said, taking it as a compliment. "I wrote it."

Ted pointed to one last box on the table. "Well,

49

maybe this will make up for that disaster." He handed it to her.

"What'd you get me?" Chris asked him. "A time bomb?"

But she gasped when she saw what was inside. "Oh, Ted, this is too much." She took out a flat, gold bracelet and held it up for everyone to see. *"To my president and first lady. Love, Ted,"* she read.

"Go ahead, put it on," he urged her.

"Ted, it's beautiful. Thank you," Chris said. The tears she was trying to hold back made her voice raspy.

"This is so you can think of me while you're busy with your meetings."

"I don't need this to remind me of you, but I'll take it anyway. I'm proud to have it." Turning aside, she wiped a tear from her eye. "I think I got some dust in my eye," she said.

"Go ahead and grab a shoulder," Ted said, pulling her head down so it rested on his. "It's your night and you can cry if you want."

"I will," Chris said. Monica felt Kim nudge her in the side and she followed Kim, Woody, and the rest of the party out of the room.

"I think I'd better excuse myself, too," Phoebe said. She trotted toward the kitchen with the empty boxes.

Chris looked up. "Wait a second, Pheeb. I want to thank you for the party."

"What are friends for?" answered Phoebe, shrugging.

"That reminds me. If you still want to talk to

me about the trip to New York, I'm here whenever you want me."

Phoebe smiled. "Not necessary. It's all taken care of."

"But over the phone you were so desperate."

"That was just a ruse to get you here," Phoebe said, lowering her voice to a whisper. "There hasn't been time to tell you. You'll never believe what happened. I spoke to my parents this morning, expecting them to say no, and give me lots of grief. But they didn't, they said I could go!"

"Phoebe, that's fantastic!" Chris cried. "See, you did all that worrying for nothing."

"They told me they went through a lot of soul-searching when they said I could go in the first place, so I didn't have to reconvince them I'd be safe with Woody's mom as a chaperone. And as far as missing school goes, they admitted that my grades are good, that I've hardly been absent all year, and that missing two days won't kill me. So everything's all set!"

Chris said, "I'm so glad everything's working out for all of us."

Phoebe winked. "I'll leave you two lovebirds alone now, and see how my guests are doing."

After throwing the boxes in the garbage, Phoebe took a couple of six-packs of soda out of the refrigerator and set them up on a table in the living room. Then she opened a can up for herself as Jake Morrell approached the table. "Great party, Phoebe," he said, reaching for a potato chip.

"Glad you could come, Jake." He was an old friend since elementary school. The six-footer's red hair was exactly the same shade as Phoebe's, and their teachers always thought they were related. "You here alone?"

"I can't stay long," he said. "I've got my history presentation due on Monday, and I've still got a lot of work left to do."

"Ugh, don't remind me," Phoebe said. "I think it's ridiculous of Mr. Novato to have us do oral reports on all the Civil War battles — in order of occurrence, no less."

"It's his favorite war," Jake said.

"That's no excuse," Phoebe added. "So what's your battle?"

"Fort Sumter. And yours?"

"The Battle of Chickamauga. I've already started my research. I'm scheduled to present on —" She gasped. "Oh no!"

"Gosh, Phoebe, what's wrong?" Jake asked.

"Nothing much," she declared. "My life is ruined, that's all."

Monica had wandered out to the patio to escape. It was unusually warm for that time of year, partly because of the thick cloud cover that hid the stars from view. The weather report had said there was a good chance of showers that evening. She hoped it would rain soon. At least then the sky would match her darkening mood.

She realized she had no one but herself to blame. She never should have put so much faith in Peter's coming to the party. But it wasn't just his no-show that was driving her crazy; it was wondering where he was. With a good-looking, outgoing guy like Peter she felt it had to mean one thing: He was out with another girl.

"Hi, Monica." Monica turned to see Sasha standing behind her. "Woody's stand-up routine too much for you?"

"It's just been one of those nights," Monica said noncommitally.

"I haven't seen you around *The Red and the Gold* office since you've been at WKND. How's it going?"

"I like it a lot. No offense, but it's more fun for me than the newspaper. The work's easy, and Peter seems to like what I'm doing."

"I'm glad, for both of you. He had an awful time of it before you came along."

"So I've heard." Trying to sound as casual as she could, Monica added, "By the way, where is Peter? I thought he'd be here."

"He would have, but he went to a concert in town. Some group called Pirate Cove. I never heard of them, but he thinks they're fantastic. He'd been waiting for this concert for months."

"Yeah, I know. He told me it was one of his favorite groups."

"I'm sure if you ask him about it on Monday, he'll tell you more than you'll ever want to know about the concert."

Monica wasn't sure about that. She was dying to know if he went alone, or with someone else, and if so, whom. But she didn't feel comfortable pressing Sasha.

Just then they heard a commotion from inside the house. "Wonder what's going on," Sasha said, rising.

Standing near the front entryway were Laurie Bennington, Dick Westergard, Gloria Macmillan, and Farley Templar.

Phoebe was reading them the riot act. "Who invited you?" she demanded.

"No one," Gloria said breezily. "We heard through the grapevine that this was where the action was, so we came to check it out."

"There's no action for you here. You're not welcome," Phoebe said.

"Oh, listen to little Miss Stuck-Up. Well, we're staying. It's a free country, isn't it?" Gloria challenged.

"Dick and I just came to offer our congratulations to Chris," Laurie said. "Believe me, Gloria is no friend of mine. Could I just speak to Chris? Please, Phoebe, I promise we'll leave afterward." She revealed a bouquet of yellow roses that she'd been holding in one hand. "I want to give these to her."

Phoebe wasn't sure she heard right. "Well, all right," she said. Then she turned back to Gloria. "Please go, now," she said firmly.

Gloria grabbed Farley's hand. "We'll go, but believe me, you'll see us again." She headed straight to her car, Farley following like a puppy on a leash. Laurie whispered to Phoebe, "This was Dick's idea, not mine. I didn't realize it was an invitation-only party." She went off in search of Chris.

Phoebe walked up to Sasha and Monica. "Do you believe that? Laurie spoke to me like a real human being."

"I think I know what it is. Dick is a wizard and he's put a magic spell on her," Sasha said.

"He must have done something," Monica added. "Yesterday she came up to the radio station and acted really friendly toward Peter."

"Peter? As in Peter Lacey?" Phoebe sat down, as if to cushion the shock. "Now I've heard everything. She used to hate his guts. This day has been full of surprises."

Monica looked at the front door, certain now that Peter would not be walking through it. "I know," she said with a sigh.

Chapter 7

Today is a good day to follow through on that special project....

Monica read her horoscope with interest as she downed a glass of milk Monday morning. She smiled. If anyone ever asked, she'd deny she depended much on the daily newspaper's astrological forecast. Nevertheless, she read it religiously every morning. Most of the time she found the generalized messages too vague to really mean anything, but today's prediction struck her. She intended to pursue the project she'd begun a few days ago: She was going to find out if Peter's interest in her was imagined or real.

After Chris's party Monica was convinced that the strange, energized feeling that had come over her recently had more to do with her feelings for Peter, than with her work at the station. She couldn't stop thinking about Peter, but her fantasies weren't altogether happy ones. In a way, her mind was like a door; on one side was the fantasy of being with Peter. In all of her imaginings they were at the radio station — it was the only place they had in common at the moment — but instead of playing records or talking over the air, Peter was holding her in his arms, spinning her around on the stool as if she were on her own personal merry-go-round. But then her mind would do a flip-flop and she'd see Peter in the seats at the Capitol Centre, watching a concert with his arm wrapped around a girl's shoulder. Monica kept trying to get a clear picture of the girl's face, but every time she got nearer, her mind obscured the image. All she knew was that the girl wasn't she, and it made her feel jealous. She still had not learned whether Peter was with a girl at the concert. But she knew it was silly to think a boy like Peter couldn't have a date every Saturday if he wanted one.

After finishing her breakfast Monica ran upstairs to her corner bedroom and got dressed. She decided she might as well do all she could to make the stars work in her favor. She put on her favorite dress, hot pink with a slim waistline, which she cinched tightly with a wide black leather belt. She liked the way the dress made her look, emphasizing her trim waist. She was going to wear her heels, but thought twice about it and changed into her open-toed black flats. She had nearly tripped once over a hole in the station's carpeting, and she didn't want to risk a repeat performance.

Monica was a model of efficiency during the twelve o'clock shift. Except for a smile when she came in, and the few requests he barked at her, Peter acted as if she was invisible. All of his energy was focused on the show, but that didn't help soothe Monica's hurt feelings. After their easygoing conversation on Friday, she had expected more from him today than a friendly hello. As the show was drawing to a close she felt as if she were going to cry. She began to wonder if she had imagined the warmth she had sensed in Peter on Friday, and felt silly when she recalled her weekend fantasies. If she hadn't known she was going to see him after school, when he couldn't hide behind the turntable, she would have felt even worse.

"I'm here." Monica knocked on the door to the station as she let herself in that afternoon.

Peter was leaning over one of the turntables, changing the needle. "I'll be with you in a second," he called out. "Routine maintenance."

Monica sighed. There was nothing ordinary about the way Peter looked. He was dressed in a steel-blue oversized pullover and off-white pleated pants. She'd seen the same outfit on a mannequin at L'Express, but Peter was no mannequin. "I'll be in the library," she told him. "There's something I want to talk to you about."

Monica smiled to herself as she noticed Peter turn his head around curiously, but she was already heading toward the record closet. If Peter was interested in her, she had realized since the lunchtime program, it was because her real interest in the station set her apart from other girls. It was silly to try to dress in hot outfits like Laurie Bennington and expect Peter to notice. If he had wanted Laurie, he could have had her. So Monica was prepared to show Peter that she was dedicated to WKND. No longer would she be bashful about her ideas to improve the station.

As Monica waited for Peter, she sat down in the library. On the floor was a large cardboard box with a California postmark on it — the shipment of records Peter had told her about on Friday. She tried to open it with a fingernail, but the strapping tape wouldn't budge. She headed back to the studio. "Is there a razor blade in here? I can't open the box."

Peter pointed distractedly to a box under the control panel. "In there. I can't guarantee it's sharp, though."

Monica bent down to rummage through the box. She had to fix her dress a few times to make sure it didn't rise too high on her legs. She laughed at herself. No one would seriously dress this way to work at a radio station. The box contained all kinds of paraphernalia like needles and cartridges, toggle switches, dust rags, wire, and a few tools. Down at the bottom she found a single-edged blade, partially covered with rust. Gingerly she carried it back to the library. It was barely sharp enough to cut through the tape.

Monica took out the records and began to file them on the shelves. Peter joined her a few minutes later. "Uh, what did you want to talk about?" he asked. He bent down and took a record out of the box.

"I got an idea over the weekend I'd like to share with you. What if, say once a week or so, you invite someone from school to perform on the radio? There's lots of talent around here — like your friends Phoebe and Woody, for instance."

Peter looked at her strangely. "I don't know how that would go over with everyone," he said skeptically. "People like to listen to me play rock 'n' roll." He held out the album in his hand. "Speaking of which, they sent me the new High Tickets album. Want to hear it?"

"Sure," Monica said, following him out to the studio. "Don't get me wrong, Peter, I think what you're doing here is fabulous. But, I also think the show would be more fun to listen to if you did something offbeat every once in a while. It doesn't have to be the WKND amateur slot, if you don't like that. I just suggested it as a way of getting other people to participate."

"I didn't say I didn't like the idea," Peter explained. "I'm just not sure about the rest of the school. I'll think about it." He set the new needle down on the album and quickly faded up the volume control knob. The loud, jarring effect of a solo guitar chord filled the room. Peter turned the monitor down to a more comfortable listening level. "To tell you the truth, I've been thinking of ways to spice up the show. All the really good jocks in D.C. are always coming up with new ideas. They all do more than just play music."

Monica had started back to the record library. "I wouldn't have even made the suggestion. But

I read 'The Ten Commandments of Disc Jockeys,' and it says a DJ should always be on the lookout for something new."

"I couldn't have said it better myself," Peter said, following her out of the studio. "I'm curious, though. What made you think of Phoebe and Woody?"

"They sang at Chris's party Saturday night," she told him. "It was corny, but sort of amusing. It reminded me of the Follies last fall, which made me think of some of the musical talent we've got at Kennedy."

"You were at the party?"

Monica could hear the surprise in his voice. "Didn't you think I would be invited?" she blurted out.

Peter rushed toward the library. "Of course — " He was looking at her, not at where he was going, and tripped over the hole in the carpet. He grabbed the closet door handle to break his fall. As he stumbled into the record library, the door closed behind him.

"Sorry," Peter apologized. His eyes darted frantically around the room. "It can get pretty hot in here with the door closed." He reached for the gold-colored doorknob, and turned it. And turned it. And turned it. The door wouldn't budge. "Let me push," he told her. He leaned his right shoulder against the door and pressed with all his strength. Nothing happened.

"We're locked in," he announced helplessly.

Monica felt he had stated the obvious. As soon as she heard the clang of the lock catching she knew what had happened. They were trapped, locked inside a tiny closet not much bigger than an elevator car. What tools they had were on the other side of the door. Most school personnel had left for the day. They were alone.

Monica looked over at Peter again. She had been presented with the opportunity she was waiting for. She was on a desert island, with the number one person on her list. Sighing contentedly, she picked up an album from the box.

Peter, meanwhile, was beating frantically on the door. "Let us out," he called several times. All he managed to do was make his fists red. "We're trapped," he said, facing the wall.

"You never can find a janitor when you need one," Monica quipped, her voice noticeably calmer than his.

"The janitor. That's it," Peter said, snapping his fingers. "He always comes in to clean up around four o'clock." He checked his watch as he turned to face Monica. "That gives us about half an hour. Hey, what are you doing?" he asked her.

"My job," she answered, putting away another record. "That's why you asked me to come by this afternoon, isn't it?"

Peter smiled. "I guess so," he said. "But aren't you afraid? It's kind of cramped in here."

Monica shook her head. "I stopped being afraid when I realized we wouldn't run out of oxygen." She pointed to the crack under the door. "I was planning on putting these records away, anyway. The only difference now is that the door's closed."

"You're amazing, Monica," Peter said.

"You're not afraid, are you, Peter?"

"No . . . well, maybe a little," he admitted. "I'm feeling claustrophobic. I know it doesn't make sense. When I close the door to the studio, I'm in a space no bigger than this. But that door has a window in it."

"It's not like we're going to be trapped in here forever," she said, trying to hide her disappointment that he wasn't delighted with the prospect of being alone with her. "Maybe if you keep busy you can keep your mind off the situation."

"You're right," he said, kneeling down to pick up some records. As he began filing he told her, "I didn't know you'd be at Chris's party."

"Kim and Woody asked me." She ventured ahead. "I thought you'd be there."

"I felt bad about missing it. I wanted to go, but I was at the Pirate Cove concert."

"I know, Sasha told me. How was it?"

"Fantastic," Peter said, the excitement of the concert reflected in his voice. "I've waited months to get to see them. I hope Chris wasn't too disappointed I didn't show."

"I think she was too overwhelmed with who was there to notice who wasn't," Monica said. "Ted gave her a beautiful bracelet."

"Really?" Peter noted. "I'm not surprised. He's hooked on her."

"It was a very romantic moment," she said. "Too bad you missed it. So you had a good time at the concert?"

"Yeah. It would have been better if I hadn't

gone alone. It's always more fun when you share an experience like that with others. You know what I mean?"

"Well, I haven't been to many concerts," she told him.

"We'll have to do something about that," Peter said. "The crowd and I get together every once in a while for a concert. Come along with us the next time we do."

It wasn't exactly a date, Monica realized, but she'd take it for now. At least she knew he hadn't been to the Pirate Cove concert with another girl. "I'd like that," she said.

Monica emptied the record box and nestled in a corner of the closet. "Do you ever think of anything besides music and radio?" she wondered aloud.

Peter finished filing the last of the records and joined her on the floor. He started to answer quickly, then stopped short. Monica didn't catch what he started to say. ". . . I guess I don't," he told her. "Everybody always tells me I'm obsessive about WKND, and the sad truth is they're right. But I wouldn't have it any other way."

"I don't blame you," she said. "If you're ever going to make it to the top you've got to go after it with a kind of concentration that lots of people just don't understand."

"You seem to understand," he said.

"I think I'd like a career in broadcasting someday," she told him. "Just being around this station has convinced me of that. I wasn't going to tell you this, but the other day, before you came, I was practicing speaking into the microphone."

Peter looked into Monica's sparkling hazel eyes and said without hesitation, "You're too pretty for radio. A girl with your looks should be thinking about TV."

Monica raised her hands to her head and laughed to hide the uneasiness that suddenly overcame her. "Yeah, sure. I can see me now. 'This is Monica Ford bringing you this latest exclusive video on MTV. . . .'" She giggled nervously.

"Hey, don't laugh. It can happen if you really want it to."

Monica paused a moment. "Maybe I'm laughing because two years ago the thought of even looking into a TV camera gave me the spooks. I used to be very shy. But part of the way I got over it was talking out loud into my cassette recorder at home. That led to mimicking DJs I heard on the radio, which finally led me to the conclusion that if they could do it, so could I."

"You did that, too? So did I, only I started when I was about eight. That's when I first got into music. I tried taking guitar lessons, but that didn't work out. So I got into the next best thing, playing songs. I've never wanted to do anything else."

"Would you want to be a VJ?" she asked. "You've got the right look."

He shook his head vigorously. "I can be so much more creative on radio — at least I could be, with the right equipment. What I wouldn't give to have a cart machine or even one reel-to-reel tape deck! Which brings us back to your earlier suggestion. I think I'll take you up on that challenge. At least I'll try it out and see what the response is." Peter took a deep breath. "Thanks for caring."

If only you knew how much, Monica wanted to say. "Thanks, Peter," she said. She had to look away from the intensity of his gaze.

Peter Lacey was having a hard time figuring out what was happening to him. A half-hour earlier he couldn't have stood the thought of being locked inside this closet. Now, he realized he was enjoying himself. For the first time since they'd met he had time to notice that his new assistant was not only smart, but also a strikingly pretty girl. To his amazement he wanted to learn all about her, and not just about her career aspirations. "It's funny, Monica, I thought I knew most of the juniors at Kennedy, but I never ran into you until now. Where have you been hiding?"

She shrugged. "It's easy to fall into the cracks at Kennedy. It's a pretty big school. We've gone through three years together and we've never had the same classes."

"It's a shame," Peter said. "Look at what I've been missing." Peter took a deep breath, trying to stop himself from saying anything more. "I'm sorry, Monica, I — I — "

Monica looked up at him. Suddenly Peter knew he couldn't resist her.

"Monica, I haven't felt like this about a girl in a long, long time." Leaning over he took her in his arms and embraced her tenderly. Then he slowly pressed his lips on hers and kissed her. Monica responded by throwing her arms around him and holding him tightly.

"Oh, Peter, I can't believe this," she whispered as soon as their lips parted.

"I'm sorry, Monica." Peter began to turn away. This isn't right, he thought to himself, it's not fair to Monica. Yet he couldn't deny the genuine delight he felt from their kiss.

"There's nothing to be sorry about," she told him. "I like you, too, Peter." She rested her head on his shoulder. Peter was unable to control the impulse to kiss her again.

They were still locked in their embrace when they were startled into attention by a sudden whoosh of fresh air. All of a sudden they were confronted with a close-up look at the janitor's scruffy work boots. They both raised their eyes at the same time. The middle-aged man's Cheshire-cat grin indicated he had seen everything.

Immediately, Peter let go of Monica and rose to his feet. She got up and concentrated on straightening her dress. Peter wasn't sure whether he wanted to murder the janitor for cutting short one of the best moments of his life, or thank him for rescuing him from one of the most dangerous.

Monica Ford, however, was *quite* sure.

Chapter 8

Phoebe dreaded making the phone call, but she had no choice. Mr. Novato had put her in a hole she couldn't get out of. Through tear-filled eyes she pressed the buttons on the touch-tone phone and called Griffin.

He answered on the first ring. Phoebe gasped. She had half hoped he wouldn't be there, so she could delay telling him her awful news. Pulling on the phone cord, she whispered in a hesitant voice, "Griffin, it's me, Phoebe."

"I'd recognize your voice anywhere," he chirped back. "I'm on my way to rehearsal so I can't talk long. But I'm glad you called."

"Don't be so sure of that. I've got bad news," she blurted out. Better to get it over with, she figured. "I can't come to New York."

"I think there's something wrong with this line. I heard you say you can't come up here. But I've got to be wrong, right?"

"No, Griffin. Oh, I can't believe what happened. My parents said it's okay for me to come up during the week, but now my history teacher's giving me grief. I've got this special project due next Wednesday, and he won't let me miss it."

Phoebe tugged on the phone cord again. When she let go, the white coil twisted around itself over and over. She started to unravel it, grateful to have something to occupy her nervous fingers.

"What's he doing — ordering you to school at gunpoint?"

"Well, no," Phoebe said. "But it's an oral report, and he won't let me present it on any other day. We're all doing Civil War battles, and he's making us present them in order. He won't accept any excuses. Believe me, I tried. So you see, I'm sunk."

"Not necessarily," Griffin said.

"What do you mean?"

"Think creatively. You're dealing with a relic from the stone age, so you know you've got more of a brain than he does. All you have to do is use it."

"You're losing me, Griffin."

"Hold on a sec. I've got an idea. The main reason you've got to present this report on Wednesday is so he doesn't get his battles mixed up, right? Why don't you just switch with someone else, and have them present your report on Wednesday?"

"Part of my grade is based on the presentation."

"So present the other person's report."

Phoebe thought a moment. "It might work,"

she reasoned. "But only if I can get someone to switch with me."

"Do you want to see me?" he asked.

"You know I do."

"Then you'll find someone," Griffin said. "When you want something badly enough — "

"I know, you get it done," she finished for him. "I've got to run now. I've got lots of phone calls to make. See you next week — I hope," she said.

"You will," he corrected. "I love you."

"I love you, Griffin."

Monica found Kim waiting for her at her locker after school Tuesday. "What are you doing here?" she cried out.

Kim slipped her index finger through a loop on her black jeans. "Is that how you greet all your friends?" Kim snickered. "I'd hate to be one of your enemies."

"I'm sorry," Monica said, chagrined. "I was just surprised to see you. I'm in kind of a hurry." She twisted her combination lock around, but when she yanked on it, it wouldn't open. "Don't these things ever work?" she said under her breath.

"I hardly ever get to see you in school anymore since you became Miss WKND. Come on over to the sub shop with me. Let's catch up on all the news."

Monica shook her head. She got the lock opened, then neatly placed her notebook on top of the history and trigonometry texts inside. "Can't, Kim. I've got to stop off at the radio station."

"Then meet me there when you're done."

"I'd like to, but I may be at the station for a while."

"Boy, Peter sure is working you hard."

"I'd hardly call it work," Monica said. "Listening to my favorite songs, joking around with Peter. In fact, he's going to show me how to run the board." She crossed her fingers behind her. Peter hadn't actually said he would take the time to work with her, but after what had happened the day before Monica didn't think he'd balk at the prospect.

"You two are spending a lot of time together."

"It doesn't seem like it. We hardly get time to speak to one another during the shows. The only time we're really together is after school."

"To work, you mean."

"Yes, work, and — " Monica hesitated. "I wasn't going to tell anyone about this, because I still don't believe it myself. Peter kissed me yesterday."

Kim's face fell. "You're kidding, right?" she asked.

Monica was puzzled. "Hey, don't take it the wrong way. I wanted him to. Remember Chris's party? See, Peter's the guy I was looking for. I didn't want to say anything because of all the fuss I made about not being interested in him. But I just can't help myself, he's irresistible."

"Let me give you some words of advice. I know you haven't had a lot of experience with guys, especially one like Peter. Just be careful."

"Kim, I know all about Peter's romantic past. But I think this is something special."

"Look, Monica, maybe Peter's being straight with you. I'm not really close to him, so I don't know. But remember, if things with Peter get messy, it will be hard to keep working at WKND. Keep your eyes open at all times."

Monica thought Kim was overreacting. If Peter had more experience than she did, it didn't matter so long as they both cared about each other. "Listen, Kim, I'm not dumb. I know what I'm doing." She started to walk down the long, narrow corridor. "Now, if you'll excuse me, Peter's waiting for me."

A few minutes later Monica threw open the door to the radio station. From the entryway she could see Peter looking over some records in the music library. She sighed. He was dressed in a funky pair of red pants and matching suspenders. She wanted to run up and give him a great big hug, but she held back. It was too early to be that free and casual about their relationship.

Peter hadn't noticed her arrival, so she marched into the library and shouted playfully, "That's my job you're doing."

He turned around quickly, and dropped a Tina Turner record. Monica thought he looked a little embarrassed, like a boy caught with his hand in a cookie jar. "I didn't expect to see you here now." He picked up the album.

"Don't you remember? You said you'd show me how to use the control board."

"I didn't mean today," he said stiffly. "I thought we'd do it some other time."

Monica was crestfallen. They had both been all business during the lunchtime show, but this wasn't the kind of greeting she'd expected. "Well, then, I guess I'd better go." She looked down at her purple polished toenails, visible through her cutaway flats. It was a strange time to notice a chipped nail on her big toe, but it was easier for her to concentrate on than Peter's puzzling behavior.

A moment later she started to turn back toward the door, but Peter stopped her, putting his hand on her shoulder. She felt his touch all the way down to the chipped toenail. "No, wait," he told her. "Please don't go. You caught me by surprise, that's all. I'm glad to see you."

"You are?"

Peter flashed a friendly smile. "Sure. And now's as good a time as any for a studio lesson." He extended his right arm in front of her. "After you, Monica."

He continued talking as they pulled up two stools next to the control panel. "I ran into Phoebe between sixth and seventh periods, and I asked her if she'd like to sing on the show. She told me she'd think about it."

"That's great — " Monica began.

Peter held up a hand. "I wouldn't book the time yet. She wasn't exactly overjoyed about the offer. In fact, she seemed a little out of it to me, like she had an awful lot on her mind."

"Well, I've heard she's got this boyfriend in New York she's going to be seeing next week. She probably misses him a lot."

"I can relate to that," Peter said. Quickly he bent down to retrieve a set of headphones from the drawer. He busied himself plugging the headphone cord into a jack on the control board and turning a few dials. "There," he said. "We're ready to rock 'n' roll." He handed Monica the headphones. "Put these on." Then he pointed to the board. "You turn this switch to the right to activate the microphone, and this knob over here to control the output level." He indicated a small black dial right under the toggle switch. It had a tiny little arrow on it. "This is the pot. Now start talking into the mike and see what happens when you play around with this level." He maneuvered the microphone to a position about six inches away from Monica's mouth.

"What should I say?" Monica asked. As she talked, she noticed the needle in the meter in the middle of the board start to waver.

"Whatever you want," Peter said. "It's your show."

Monica picked up on the cue. "Well, then, let me say this is Monica Ford, bringing you all the latest hits on WKND, the voice of Kennedy High."

"Hey, not bad. You've got a great voice," Peter said. "But what you want to do is keep that little needle out of that red area," he continued, pointing to the meter. "You were in it a lot. If you'd been on the air, your voice would have been too distorted to understand. This knob will control the level."

"Got you, chief," she said.

Monica set up her own record, with Peter showing her the controls that turned on the turntable from the board. "Now you're set. Let's hear you intro a record."

Monica flashed an okay sign, then focused all her concentration on the board. "Good afternoon, everyone, this is The Monica Ford Show. Today we've got a special treat for you, something I know you're going to like. Something hot. Something bad. Something unbelievable. It's 'Something Out There' by Tony Jones." At that exact moment she pressed the button that started the turntable. The instrumental blasted out of the studio monitor speaker.

Peter began to keep time to the music, rapping his fingers on his thighs. But a few moments later he looked up at Monica and asked, "Want to dance?"

The invitation caught her by surprise, but she wasted no time placing the headphones on the counter and joining Peter. There wasn't much room to maneuver in the tiny booth, so they spun around and around in a circle, hands touching. Gradually they moved closer to one another, drawn inward like two magnets, until they were locked in a close embrace.

It was more than a dance to Monica; it was a confirmation that the events of the day before were no fluke. Peter's grip on her was strong and confident. She could hear the beat of his heart as she rested her head on his broad chest. She liked the way it felt to hold him. They were moving around in total harmony, as if some natural instinct enabled them to predict each other's steps. Monica couldn't see Peter's face, couldn't read his expression, but she was convinced he had to be feeling the same things she did.

They broke apart as soon as the song ended.

For a moment they stood looking at each other, neither one willing to say the first words.

Monica broke the impasse. "I've got to sign off," she said, hopping back on the stool. She flipped open the microphone switch. "Hey, everyone, that was a blast from Tony Jones. This is Monica Ford wishing you a pleasant good afternoon, but before I leave I've got one request. That's for Peter Lacey to join me at my house this Friday night for a little pizza and video. That's this Friday night, my house, at 3882 Wildwood Road."

Peter was standing directly behind her, and when he didn't respond right away Monica froze. She had been too direct. She gingerly took off the headphones and placed them on the counter.

Then she heard Peter say, "Gee, Monica, I'd like nothing better. . . ."

She spun around on the stool. Peter had his thumbs tucked under his suspenders, his head bent so low to the floor that all she could see was the top of his head. "So can I expect you around eight?"

"Monica, I'm sorry," he began, slowly lifting his eyes to hers.

"Sorry?" Monica tensed.

"I'm sorry, I won't be able to make it till eight-thirty. Will that be okay?"

Monica's entire body relaxed. "Sure, great."

He slapped his hands together. "I think we're wrapped up in here for the day. Let's close up shop."

Monica didn't say anything else until Peter locked the front door to the station and they began to walk down the long hallway. "Peter, I didn't put you on the spot back there, did I?"

"No," he said. "I was just thinking. It's been a long time since I've done anything but hang out with the guys on Friday nights."

"So I've upset a long-standing routine?"

"I wouldn't really put it that way. It's a habit I don't mind breaking. But let's keep it our little secret — just for the time being. I made such a big stink about never dating any of my assistants, I know I'd be in for a lot of razzing from my friends if they knew."

"Well, okay," Monica agreed reluctantly. "While I'm thinking about it, what kind of pizza shall I order?"

"Anything you like. I'll eat any kind of pizza in the world. Even whole wheat."

"I never ate one of those."

"One of Sasha's concoctions. It's one of the few things I'll eat at her house. They're the grossest-looking pizzas you'd ever want to see. But they taste pretty good."

"I think I'll stick to the regular kind."

"I've got an even better idea. Let's go out for pizza, instead. I know a great place. Then we can go back to your place or mine, and watch TV or something."

"My mom's always out on Friday nights, so we could have the family room VCR all to ourselves. What kind of movies do you like?"

"Anything except heavy shoot-'em-ups," he said. "I'm the nonviolent type."

"Me, too," Monica said. "I'll rent something fun."

They'd reached the parking lot, heading in the direction of Peter's ancient but reliable Volkswagen bug. "May I offer you a ride home?" he asked.

Monica pointed to a white Toyota. "That's mine — a guilt present from my father. Ever since he and my mom got divorced he's been buying me gifts. I keep telling him he doesn't have to, but he won't listen." She shrugged. "I guess I shouldn't complain."

"Hi, Peter, Monica." Chris was waving her arms as she ran across the parking lot to catch up with them. "Working late at the radio station?"

"Just catching up on old business," Peter said.

"I'm coming from an Honor Society meeting myself. Can I bum a ride home?"

"Sure," Peter said.

"Well, I'd better be going," Monica said. "See you tomorrow."

As she began to walk away she couldn't help overhearing Chris say to Peter, "Phoebe got a letter from Lisa. Did she tell you?"

Monica listened. She knew — everybody at Kennedy knew — that Lisa Chang, a locally famous ice skater, was a good friend of Phoebe's. But she didn't know why Peter would be especially interested in her letter to Phoebe. It would have been awkward to turn around and ask, so she kept walking. Still, she kept her ears open for Peter's response. But he didn't say anything, at least not anything audible. The next thing she heard was the sound of his car door slamming shut.

Monica forced herself not to dwell on it. She

focused on the good news: She had a date with Peter on Friday. Lisa was probably one of twenty girls who had a crush on Peter. Of course Chris would put in a good word for a friend. Besides, Lisa Chang was two thousand miles away in Colorado. Monica Ford would be sitting right next to Peter every day for the rest of the school year.

Chapter
9

Phoebe sat in the booth at Bradley's Creamery that afternoon, staring at the hot fudge sundae in front of her. In preparation for her trip she'd gone on a crash diet, and had lost five pounds. She knew she risked putting them all back on, with this dieter's nightmare, but right then she didn't care.

Defiantly, she dug into the glass bowl. The cool strawberry ice cream was a heavenly escape from the disaster her life had become. As she reached for her second spoonful she looked up and saw a bright pink and green Hawaiian shirt, dotted with little coconuts. Only one person she knew owned a shirt like that. "Hi, Woody," she said. "If you've come to ask me a favor, the answer is no." She felt like an overloaded electric circuit. If someone tried to plug in one more thing she thought she'd explode.

Woody slid into the oak booth across the table from her. Kim was right behind him. "What side of the bed did you wake up on this morning, Miss Grouchface?"

"I'm warning you, don't start with me. . . ."

"This doesn't sound like the Pheeberooni I know and love. Care to tell old Doctor Woody about your problem?"

"Which one?" she asked.

"Oh, dear," Woody said. "I'm going to need some fortification." He smiled at the approaching waitress. "Donna," he said, speedreading her nameplate, "I need a banana split with all the trimmings. Kim?" He looked to his girl friend.

"I'll have a diet cola."

"That's inhuman," Woody said. Then he asked Phoebe, "Are you still having trouble finding someone to help you with your history project?"

She nodded. "I called every kid in my class. Mr. Novato's put such a scare into everyone that they've practically finished their research. And, naturally, they want to present their own reports."

"Everybody?"

"Well, there's one exception. This guy Howard Walker. He's a real jerk, hardly ever shows up in class. He said he'd switch with me."

"That's good news, isn't it?" Kim asked.

"No. He hasn't even started his research — which means I'm going to have to start from scratch. And he'll only do it if I hand him a finished presentation, so now I'll have to do two entire reports. And if that isn't bad enough, his is scheduled for the day I get back from New

York, so I've got to have both ready before I leave." She shoved a huge spoonful of ice cream into her mouth.

"You can do it," Woody said.

"Sure, if I lock myself in my room all weekend," Phoebe grumbled.

"Pheeberooni, don't you see what this means? You're free to go to New York. That's what counts, isn't it? Years from now, you'll remember your rendezvous with Griffin, and you'll have forgotten about all the hassles you had to go through."

"Yeah, you're right." She could always count on Woody to put things in their proper perspective. "But that's not all. I ran into Peter this afternoon. He's got this crazy idea about me singing on the radio."

"What's so crazy about that?" Woody asked. "I think it shows the old boy's got some brains in his head. It's about time he let some of his friends get in on a little radio action."

"He wants me to be his first guinea pig. I can't do it," Phoebe wailed.

"Did you tell him no?" Kim wondered.

"I said I'd think about it."

Woody stared at her. "If you're really against it, why didn't you turn him down on the spot?"

Phoebe didn't like the way Woody was examining her, as if she were something under a microscope. "I was in a hurry, okay?" she said, waving her hands in the air.

Woody shook his head back and forth, like one of those spring-necked dogs people put in the rear window of their cars. "You're going to have to do better than that, Pheeb. I know an excuse when I smell one."

"What's it to you, Webster?" she challenged.

"I happen to be your number one fan. I don't give a hoot who came up with the idea, but I'd sell my entire collection of Frank Sinatra records to hear you sing on the radio."

"That's very thoughtful of you, but —" She stopped short and cried out, "Woody, you don't even have any Frank Sinatra records!" There he goes again, she thought, her mouth forming a smile even though her brain was telling it to pout. Woody always came up with some ridiculous statement he knew would make her smile.

"That's beside the point. I want you to get on the phone right now and tell Peter you'll do it."

"I can't."

"Can't call or can't sing?"

"I can't sing on the radio — can I?"

"You're the girl who wowed them at the Follies, remember? In your saner moments, you've even admitted how itchy you are to sing again. So what's stopping you?"

"I'm scared," she admitted.

"Pheeb, in the words of one of our immortal presidents — I forget which one — 'You have nothing to fear but fear itself.' "

"I just thought of something that might convince you," Kim said. "If you go on and sing a song, tape it for Griffin. Then you could surprise him with the tape when you see him."

"Well, I don't know. . . ."

"I've heard you worrying about whether Griffin will still be impressed with you. This is a great way to show him your stuff," Kim said.

Woody grabbed Kim in a bear hug. "You're so smart. How come I didn't think of that?" Turning to Phoebe he announced, "That does it, you're singing. I'll even accompany you on guitar. I don't think my piano will fit in the studio."

Phoebe held up her hands. Usually she rebelled when people tried to gang up on her like this, but she was in no mood to fight. Deep down she knew Woody and Kim were right; this was too good an opportunity to pass up. "Okay, I'll do it," she said.

Somehow, now that she'd made the final decision, she felt a lot better. She took a deep breath and looked down at her half-eaten sundae. The chocolate swirls were a muddy mess, and the melting strawberry ice cream was decidedly unappetizing. She pushed away the dish.

Then with all the solemnity of a Sunday school teacher she looked back at Woody. "There's just one problem," she announced, her pale face full of worry.

"What's that?"

Now that she had his total attention she broke out into a full-faced grin. "What am I going to sing?"

"And now, live from our very own WKND studios, we have a very special treat. Our very own Phoebe Hall!"

Peter hopped off his stool and made room for

Phoebe next to the control board. Leaning over her shoulder he positioned the microphone between her and Woody, who was already seated on another stool.

"Thank you, Peter," Phoebe said, hoping her nerves didn't show in her voice. She knew she couldn't be seen, but she'd taken great pains to look nice. She was wearing her lucky jeans, the ones with more pockets than a billiards table, and a white silk blouse, with a large green sash tied around her waist. She'd even thought to put on tiny gold button earrings instead of the long, dangling ones she preferred, so that they wouldn't clang and be picked up through the microphone as she moved her head.

Taking a deep breath, she plunged ahead. "This song is dedicated to everyone who's ever fallen in love . . . or who has wanted to. Ready, Maestro?" She gave Woody a little shove. It wasn't the smoothest way to cue him to begin, she realized, but it was effective. Woody winked back and began to strum.

The song Phoebe had chosen was a ballad. She heard it on the radio the night she had decided to do this show, and felt it was perfect. The song always made her think of Griffin. Even now, as she sang the first few words, she pictured his boyish grin and the way his brown hair flopped down on his forehead when he got excited.

Somehow, just thinking of Griffin helped make the words more meaningful to her. She sang with such intensity and power, Peter had to rush back into the studio and readjust the volume levels he'd preset earlier. She was going too much into the red.

Peter retreated back to the record library, where Monica was perched on the floor, her portable cassette recorder straddling her legs. A long wire connected it to the back of the control panel. Because the doors between the studio and the library were open Monica had to keep quiet. All she could do was smile as Peter sat down beside her, his red and white argyle socks a perfect complement to her red and white polkadot anklets. Monica took it as an omen that things would work out fine during their date that evening.

During the course of the song Peter moved closer to her. At first his move was almost imperceptible, but there was no denying it when he placed his arm gently on her shoulder. He was so close Monica could hear him breathing. She had to stop herself from reaching over to touch him.

The mood was shattered with the final notes of Woody's guitar. Immediately, Peter bolted up and headed back to the studio. He didn't want to run the risk of having any dead air, in case Phoebe didn't have anything else to say. Monica refused to let it bother her. She knew she'd get her turn that evening.

After Phoebe introduced Woody, Peter quickly grabbed the mike and thanked both of them for coming. He'd timed it so they'd end his show, so he said, "And that's all for today, folks. Tune in next week for more surprises. *Ciao!*" With that he signed off.

As soon as the red light went out, Phoebe yelped with relief. "I never thought I'd make it. How did I sound?"

"Fantastic," Peter said, patting her on the back. "You really know how to belt out a song."

Monica came into the studio, holding the cassette recorder in her hand. "Do you want to hear it now?" she asked.

Phoebe shook her head, holding out her hands. "Look how I'm shaking. I think I'm more nervous now that it's over."

"Typical show business remark," Woody commented.

"Griffin's going to be proud of you," Monica added, as she removed the tape from the recorder and put it back into its box. She handed it to Phoebe.

"I hope so," Phoebe said. She was clutching the box so hard her knuckles were turning white. "I'm not going to tell him about this till I see him. Five days and counting."

Eight hours and counting, Monica thought to herself. She felt she understood Phoebe's excitement and anxiety better than anyone else in the room.

Chapter
10

At exactly eight-thirty, Peter pulled his Volkswagen up in front of the Fords' colonial-style house.

Monica was alone and she had seen him walking up the path from her second-story bedroom window. He had changed since that afternoon and was now wearing electric blue pants, a red shirt, yellow unconstructed blazer, and black Reeboks.

She looked down at her own outfit, a baby-blue, bibbed overall and white sweater. She hoped he wouldn't think she was underdressed, but she had gone for a deliberately casual appearance. Oh well, she sighed, it was too late to change. Jumping off her chair she hopped down the twelve steps to the front door. "Hi, there," she chirped.

She watched as Peter's eyes appraised her outfit. "Hi, yourself. You look great, Monica."

"Thanks. Ditto," she said. "I don't know about you, but I'm hungry."

"What are we waiting for? Let's go." Peter offered an arm, which Monica gladly looped with her own.

When they got to the intersection at Rose Hill's main street, Peter smiled slyly, and made a right turn toward Route 495. Monica was puzzled. "I thought we were going to Mario's."

Peter talked as he kept his eyes fixed on the road. "I said I was taking you out for pizza. Now I know everyone in Rose Hill thinks Mario's is the only place in the world that makes a decent pie, but I know a place that's even better."

"In Washington?"

"Bethesda," he said confidently. "A little hole in the wall not too far away from the Navy complex. The story I heard was that some admiral found this guy in Sicily, and brought him over here as his very own chef. Then one day the guy had a fight with the admiral and set up his own shop. I don't know how true that is, but the pizza's pretty good."

"So's the story," Monica added. "Do you go there often?"

"Only on special occasions."

Monica smiled. It was heartwarming to be thought of as a special occasion. "I thought Phoebe was great today."

Peter nodded. "I was going to credit you on the air for having come up with the idea, but in all the excitement I forgot. I'm sorry."

"Hey, nothing to be sorry for. It was just an idea."

"But new ideas are what keep radio shows lively. Did you catch what I said in my closing about having some surprises next week?"

"Yes," Monica said, remembering. "Care to clue me in?"

"I think I'd better, since it involves you directly. Next Friday you're going to DJ the show."

For a moment, Monica didn't know what to say. Peter was more possessive of his show than a mother with a newborn baby. "I'm honored," she told him. "But why?"

"Don't you want to do it?"

"Of course I do. But I never thought you'd let anyone else DJ the show."

Peter took his eyes off the steady stream of traffic ahead of them and gave her a smile. "Boy, when a guy gets a reputation it's hard to change it. I know the whole school sees me as this crazed guy whose life is focused on that little booth." He paused. "To some extent they're right. I love my show more than anything in the world. But that doesn't mean I'm blind to other people's ambitions. I've seen how much you love radio, too. I have no right to hog the airwaves and keep you off just to satisfy my ego. You deserve a chance, too."

A few minutes later, they arrived at the restaurant, A Taste of Italy. They were seated at a small wooden table, between a family of five and a group of older, college-aged guys. They were singing "99 Bottles of Beer on the Wall" loudly enough to be heard all the way back in Rose Hill.

Monica looked over the menu. "What do you recommend?"

Peter's nose was in the menu. He didn't respond.

"What kind of pizza are we getting?" she said, a little louder.

He looked up over his menu. "Did you say something?" he asked.

The two of them laughed, and Peter reached over to grab her hand. "I hadn't counted on being serenaded like this." He gestured toward the rowdy singers. "I hope you'll forgive me."

Peter looked apologetic, as if he'd committed a crime by bringing her to this restaurant. All Monica wanted was to spend the evening with him. They could have gone to a toxic waste dump for all she cared. At least they could eat here. Looking around her she commented loudly, "It's different. Those guys are a lot more colorful than Mario's jukebox."

Peter squeezed her hand even tighter. "You're great, Monica."

In between their neighbors' beer songs, they talked about school, the station, and Monica's upcoming stint. Monica found out they both had the same chemistry teacher, at different times of the day, and they were both having trouble balancing organic chemical formulas. She also found out they both liked to bowl, and Peter made a tentative promise to take her out to the Rose Hill Lanes some night.

But it was hard to hold up a conversation amid the surrounding noise, so as soon as they finished

91

their sausage and mushroom pizza they left. "You were right about the pizza," Monica said as they walked to the parking lot. "It's better than Mario's."

"Maybe next time we'll remember to bring earplugs," he added. "I don't know about you, but I'm ready to settle down and watch a nice, quiet movie."

Twenty minutes later they were back at Monica's house. Peter helped her make a batch of popcorn in the kitchen. Then she led him into the den and told him to make himself comfortable on the gray and white overstuffed sofa, while she set up the VCR.

Monica put the video cassette in the machine, then closed the door that separated the den from the rest of the house. No one else was home. Her mother wasn't expected back until after midnight, and her younger sister Julie was spending the night at a friend's house. But Monica liked the sense of intimacy she felt with the door closed, and if the night continued the way it was going she knew she'd be wrapped in Peter's arms before too long.

Monica held the remote control in her hand as she turned off the overhead light. The room was dark, except for the TV and the fluorescent glow of the aquarium under the far window. "I got *Romancing the Stone*. It's one of my favorite movies. Have you seen it?"

"Never got around to it."

Monica nestled into a corner of the couch and pressed the start button on the remote control. "Hope you like it."

Peter was on the other side of the seven-foot sofa, the bowl of popcorn resting on the cushion separating them. "Why are you sitting over there?" he asked. "Come on over here. I won't bite."

Monica slid over. Peter offered her some popcorn, then put the bowl between his knees. He rested his right hand on the arm of the sofa, the other arm on his lap. His gaze was directed toward the TV screen.

Monica had a hard time forcing herself to stare at the TV. She would have been content to study Peter's handsome face all evening. As it was, she had to pinch herself to make sure she wasn't fantasizing this whole date. She wasn't, but it was easy for her to imagine she was the one riding into the sunset with her love, instead of the heroine at the very beginning of the movie. Of course, the boy with her was Peter. "Have you ever been on a horse?" she asked him.

"Yeah, at summer camp when I was a kid. Never could ride like that." He pointed to the screen.

"Me, either," she said, reality creeping in on her fantasy. "The last time my dad took me riding, I fell off. They make it look so easy in the movies." She leaned over Peter's leg to grab another handful of popcorn. There was an art to eating popcorn in the company of a boy, she realized. Monica munched on one kernel at a time, making sure she didn't crunch too hard and make Peter aware of the noise.

After she took the handful, Peter moved the bowl so that it rested on his thigh. He slid back against the sofa cushions so that his head was about level with Monica's shoulder.

She turned her head back to the TV. Kathleen Turner and Michael Douglas were falling down a giant wall of mud.

"All right!" Peter cried, popping a kernel into his mouth. "That looks like more fun than the water slide at Adventure Park."

"I think I'll take the water over the mud," Monica said. "My favorite part's at the end when — "

Peter put a finger to his lips. "Don't tell me," he said. "I want to be surprised."

They didn't say anything else as they returned their attention to the movie. Monica was absorbed in the fantasy again, picturing herself as the heroine and wondering what it was like to go off to a faraway country to face danger and excitement. She'd never been west of her grandparents' house in Lexington, Kentucky.

Of course, in her mind's eye, Peter was the hero, her partner in romance and adventure. As the movie progressed she slunk down the sofa, and moved so close to him they were practically touching.

Then, when Kathleen Turner looked into Michael Douglas's eyes and proclaimed her love for him, Monica felt as if she'd been speaking for her. Just then Peter slid his left arm across her shoulders. This was the moment she'd been waiting for. She felt his movement gave her permission to bury her head under his shoulder and wrap an arm across his chest. He caressed her tighter, his fingers drawing long lines down her back.

"Oh, Peter," she whispered, "I wish we could stay like this forever. Don't you?"

Peter's hand stopped moving. He bolted upright, as if waking from a dream. The force pushed Monica against the back of the sofa and tipped over the popcorn bowl. Kernels were scattered all over the gray tweed carpet. "Oh, I'm sorry, Monica," he said. "I'll clean this mess up right now." He started to bend over, but Monica twisted her body and grabbed one of his arms.

"The popcorn can wait," she said. Peter's mood swing was as swift and unexpected as a slap in the face. "What happened, Peter? What did I do wrong?"

Peter ran a hand through his hair. "It's not you, Monica. It's me. I'm a real jerk, and if you're as smart as I think you are, you'll do yourself a favor and throw me out of the house."

"Why should I? I've been having one of the happiest nights of my life — until now."

"That's the problem. So have I." His eyes looked droopy and his mouth formed an apologetic frown.

"Since when is having a good time a problem?" she asked.

Peter eased off the sofa and paced past the wet bar to the other side of the room. He slammed his hands into his pockets, not knowing what else to do with them. "There's no easy way to tell you this. . . ."

Monica felt her nose tingle and her eyes begin

to moisten. "Did somebody put you up to this?" she rasped. "Was tonight some kind of joke?"

Peter started to move closer. Monica closed her eyes. If only, she thought, if only the last five minutes were a bad dream and I could wake up with Peter sitting next to me. But he stopped short just before he reached the sofa. He shoved his hands back in his pockets. Monica had never seen him behave so awkwardly.

"Monica, you haven't done anything. And this isn't a joke. You've got to believe me when I tell you that. I like you and I wouldn't want to hurt you for anything. That's why I got up just now. I can't go through with this and hurt you."

Kathleen Turner and Michael Douglas were still kissing, working their way toward their happy ending. It seemed so inappropriate to Monica, she reached for the remote control and turned it off. Then she rose and turned on the overhead light. There didn't seem to be any reason to inspire intimacy any longer. She sat down on the leather easy chair next to the sofa and faced Peter. "Why?" she asked.

Peter looked as if he were going to cry. "I have a girl friend," he announced.

"Who?" It was the last thing Monica had expected to hear. "Where? I haven't seen you hanging out with anybody."

"She's not here. I mean she lives here, but she hasn't been around for several months. Her name is Lisa Chang."

Monica winced, recalling how she had dismissed Lisa as another girl with a crush on Peter.

"I've heard of her," she said blankly. "The ice skater."

"She's at a training center in Colorado. We've been writing back and forth ever since she left."

Monica felt numb. It was the only way she could cope with the news. "I remember now. You interviewed her on your show last fall. You sounded as if you hated her."

Peter nodded, a bemused expression forming on his face. "You have a fantastic memory. I didn't like her then, but that was before I knew her. She's one of the most gentle, caring people I know."

Monica held up her hand. "Please don't, Peter."

"Of course," Peter said apologetically. "But that's part of the reason I'm so confused. I like you, Monica. I didn't lie about that when I kissed you that day we got locked in the closet, and I didn't lie about wanting to be with you tonight. But I feel like I'm caught in a vise. Lisa and I promised we'd wait for each other, and not date anyone else. I broke that promise because I care about you. But because I care about you, I can't let this go any further." He shrugged helplessly. "Does any of this make sense?"

"What do you want me to say — yes?" Monica asked. "I feel miserable."

"So do I," Peter said. "I'd call Lisa up right now and tell her I want to break up with her. But as her friend I can't do it. She practicing for the tryouts for the national team. It means the world to her, and it would be horrible of me to break this kind of news to her now. I can't do that."

"Oh, Peter. I understand what you're saying, and if I were you I'd do the same thing. But you can't expect me to be happy about it." Monica felt as if someone else were talking. Every impulse inside her was telling her to scream, kick, and throw things around. But she couldn't.

"I don't," Peter said. "I thought I could avoid the issue by dating you anyway. That's why I told you to keep this our little secret. That's why I took you to that restaurant in Bethesda tonight. I thought maybe we'd have a few out-of-town dates, by which point I'd tire of you and get back to Lisa.

"I was wrong. I realized tonight that we could have something good together. I was looking forward to coming back here, watching a good movie, and getting as close to you as I could.

"But I couldn't go through with it. I'm not a dishonest person by nature and when I saw how much you seemed to like me I knew I had to stop things before they went too far. I couldn't ask you to keep a relationship like ours a secret. That wouldn't be fair to you. I couldn't bring it out in the open by splitting up with Lisa. That wouldn't be fair to her. The only fair thing to do is to put an end to our relationship right now."

The tears were falling shamelessly down Monica's cheeks. She felt Peter should have been honest with her from the start. Their relationship had already gone beyond the completely casual stage, as far as she was concerned. Breaking up this way didn't seem fair to her. Yet she couldn't deny she admired Peter's honesty and his loyalty to Lisa.

It was all too confusing. She felt overloaded and unable to cope. "You'd better go now." She started to walk toward the door.

"I'm so sorry, Monica. You deserve a lot better," Peter said. He walked ahead of her and grabbed the doorknob. He was in a hurry to leave, too. "But before I go I want to let you know I still want you to do that show on Friday. I don't want all this to turn you off to radio. You're very talented."

Monica couldn't think about that now. "Goodbye, Peter. I'll let you know on Monday."

Peter heard the door slam behind him. This wasn't how he'd planned to end his night with Monica. But as he walked to his car, he realized he'd been acting on automatic pilot these past few days. He had been guided by his emotions, and hadn't really given much rational thought to what it meant to date Monica. He should have, he berated himself. He'd made a huge mess of things.

As soon as he got inside the car he pounded his fists on the steering wheel. He had never before wanted to be committed to any girl, always picturing himself as an independent guy. Yet here he was caught between two wonderful and very different girls.

Peter was too upset and confused to go home, so he drove down the streets of Monica's development, past the high school, through downtown toward Washington. He hadn't planned to, but a few minutes later he entered the parking lot of the Capitol Skating Rink.

Peter hadn't driven there in months, not since Lisa had left, and never before on a Friday night. The parking lot was fuller than he'd ever seen it — Lisa skated during the off hours, when only the truly serious skaters were on the ice. He waited while a blue Chevy backed out of a space. There were a man and a woman inside, laughing about something. Peter shook his head. He hadn't felt further from laughing in a long time.

After parking, he walked through two rows of cars to the front entrance of the bunker-like building. It was as if he had entered another world. Rock music was blaring out of the tinny-sounding speakers, and colored lights that were never on during the day blinked back and forth over the oval rink, where a large crowd of people was moving in an endless circle.

Peter hopped onto the bleachers and stared at the skaters for a while. He thought it was strange that these people paid money to glide around for hours, as if they were on a treadmill. This wasn't skating to him. It had as much to do with what Lisa did, as playing records on an automatic turntable did with being a DJ.

Closing his eyes, he flashed back to the last time he saw Lisa skate. It was a Saturday morning, just before she left for Colorado. He even remembered what she wore: a red leotard, purple tights, and red-and-purple striped leg warmers. She was so excited. She wanted to show him a new sequence she had thought up for her short program, a series of compulsory moves she had to do during competition. Like a frisky puppy she danced onto the ice, gliding along as if it were the only mode of locomotion she'd ever known. Peter had thought the little spin she did at the start was worth a perfect six, but Lisa had chided him, explaining she was only warming up.

He understood what she meant when she actually began to skate, flying through a series of spins, axels, and jumps he thought were beyond human achievement. When she finished she came back to the rail, pouting, terribly disappointed she hadn't done her best for him. Peter remembered how he'd stared at her in disbelief; he hadn't seen any mistakes at all. Yet he knew what she meant. It was the same way with him when his transitions between songs weren't one hundred percent seamless. Nobody else caught the mistakes, but he did. Both of them were always striving for perfection.

Peter then tried to remember their last date, but the image was growing hazy and he couldn't keep her face in focus. He was having trouble remembering how it had felt to kiss her. It had been so long ago.

Shaking his head, Peter opened his eyes. A blond-haired girl he didn't know had come up to him; she asked if he wanted to skate with her. Without answering, he stood up and rushed out of the rink.

Peter decided if he was going to call himself Lisa's boyfriend, he had to have a relationship with her, not just a collection of letters, and a vague promise of seeing her again. They'd had a strong, special alliance, but it was becoming harder to know what that meant anymore.

As soon as he got home he ran to his room

and looked up Lisa's number. It was about nine-thirty in Colorado, he calculated, so there was a good chance of her being there. He got an answer on the fourth ring. "Hello, is Lisa Chang there?"

There was a momentary pause on the other end. "Peter? Peter, is that you?"

"Lisa!" Peter cried. He wondered why he hadn't recognized her hello. "How are you?"

"Tired," she answered. "I was on the ice for seven hours today. I've got my triple toe loop down so well that the coach has decided to play it up in my routine. We've changed everything around, and I've got only two weeks to make it perfect. But how are *you*, Peter? I didn't expect you to call."

"I just wanted to say I love you."

"Oh Peter, I love you, too. How are things at school? That new assistant working out for you?"

Peter felt as though Lisa could read his mind. His heart jumped to his throat. "Uh, she's fine."

"And the gang?"

"Great. I had Phoebe sing on the air today."

"You're kidding!" Lisa shrieked. "Gosh, I wish I could have heard her."

"We taped it. Phoebe's bringing it with her when she visits Griffin next week. I'll make a copy of it and send it to you."

"Maybe you won't have to." Lisa let the words hang in the air a moment before continuing. "I was going to surprise you, but now that you're on the phone I can't keep it to myself anymore. I'm coming home next weekend."

For the first time in his life Peter was struck

speechless. "When did this happen?" he managed to say after a moment's silence.

Lisa giggled. "I know. I was pretty floored myself when the coach told me he arranged for me to do an exhibition at the Capitol Skating Rink next Saturday," she said excitedly. "I just found out on Wednesday, so it's not like I've been keeping it from you for a long time."

"That's great," Peter said. But his neck felt as if someone had aimed a blowtorch on it. He rubbed it with the back of his hand. "How long will you be here?"

"Just the weekend. I'll be flying in Friday and leaving Sunday. That'll give us Friday and Saturday nights, that is, if you don't already have plans."

"Nothing I can't change for you," he told her. He wondered why he'd said that. Now that he'd stopped things with Monica, he was free to do what he wished.

"In that case, why don't you come to my house around seven?" she told him. "I can't wait to see you."

He hung up the phone, then lay back on his bed and stared at the Bruce Springsteen poster tacked up on his ceiling. Did Bruce ever have girl problems like this back in his dating days? he wondered. Probably not. A guy like Bruce was too smart to have been involved with two girls at the same time.

He sat up when he realized where his mind was taking him. He didn't have two girls to deal with anymore. He'd told Monica plain and clear that they were through — end of conflict, end of problem. He give himself a pat on the back for having thought of confessing all to Monica tonight. As sticky a situation as he had gotten himself into, it would have been much worse if he hadn't said anything, and Lisa had surprised them all, as she'd planned.

So everything was settled in a way that was fair to all of them. He and Lisa would be together, and Monica was free to pursue any other boy she wanted.

Then why, Peter asked himself, was he already dreading next weekend?

Chapter
11

Monica wondered if she'd ever feel normal again.

Ever since Peter had left her house on Friday she'd been in a daze, not quite believing what had happened to her. It just wasn't fair, she kept telling herself. All she could think of was that old saying: It's better to have loved and lost than never to have loved at all. She wanted to find the author and punch him in the nose. He had it backward. Losing Peter hurt more than all the pain she suffered during her years on the sidelines.

The realization that she fell short in his eyes was what hurt the most. But then how could she compete with an Olympic-caliber ice skater? All weekend long she tried to remember what Lisa Chang looked like. She'd seen a picture of her in *The Red and the Gold* once, but didn't think she'd actually seen her at school. Lisa had spent so little time at Kennedy that that was under-standable. But Monica thought she must be beautiful — a girl who'd hold Peter's attention so long had to be. And she had to be very nice. She couldn't imagine him falling for anyone with the cold-heartedness of a Laurie Bennington or Gloria Macmillan. It just made Monica hurt all the more.

Monica left for school Monday morning feeling sad and confused. But the one thing she knew was that she wasn't going to let this awful epi-sode spoil her work at the radio station. She hadn't joined WKND with the intention of dating Peter, and she was determined not to lose sight of her goal. As painful and awkward as it would be, she knew she had to act as if their date had never happened.

All morning long she dreaded twelve o'clock and tried to concentrate on her classes. PE was easy, and she had a French test that forced her to concentrate on her work, but when she got to trigonometry she drifted away from the lecture. She glanced up at the clock so often she called attention to herself.

"Monica," Ms. Landorf called, "have you de-cided to become a clockmaker?"

The question startled her. "N-no," she said, wondering why the rest of the class was turning to look at her.

"I'm surprised. You've been staring at that clock so intently I thought you were planning to build one. Now, would you like to tell the class the solution to problem number five?"

Monica stared down at her homework assignment. Next to the number five she'd drawn a right triangle and a huge question mark. If she didn't have the answer when she tackled this homework the night before, she wasn't going to have it now. She shrugged. "I don't know."

"Then I suggest you stop counting the seconds till this class is over and pay attention." Ms. Landorf's blue eyes cut into her like a laser. Ron Shirley snickered at her from his seat in the front row before turning back to the teacher.

Monica felt humiliated. She never spaced out in class like this, at least not in a way that would cause her to get caught. "Darn you, Peter Lacey," she muttered under her breath.

But the feeling didn't last long. As soon as she walked into the station and saw Peter bouncing up and down on his stool to the beat of Mick Jagger she knew she could never remain really angry with him. She couldn't dislike anyone with that much love of life, who had such a strong sense of loyalty he couldn't stand to hurt a girl some two thousand miles away. Monica told herself she had to take comfort in the realization that she'd still get to be with him every day, though only on a platonic level.

But talking to him was another matter. She thought about walking into the studio and saying hi before going into the record library. His looks were enhanced by an oversize azure sweat shirt that brought out the intensity of his green eyes. He was rapping his fingers on the counter-top in time to the music, almost oblivious to her presence. As she approached him, she felt a huge lump rise in her throat. She couldn't make the words come out, and as she tried her eyes began to mist up with tears of frustration. Hastily, she retreated to the library.

Monica took a tissue out of her purse and gently dabbed the inside edges of her eyes, careful not to smudge her mascara. Then she quickly refiled a few records left out from Friday's show, then reentered the studio as the Mick Jagger record was ending.

Feeling more composed she asked, "Would you like me to pull some records for you?" Her voice was as controlled and businesslike as a telephone operator's.

Peter seemed to jump when he heard her. "Hey, Monica." There was a smile on his face as he turned around. "Glad to see you. Could you get me these?" He tore off a page from his notepad and handed it to her.

Monica was careful not to let her hand touch his. "With pleasure," she said. She hoped the words didn't sound as hollow to Peter as they did to her. She left the studio, kicking the door closed behind her.

How could he do that? Monica thought miserably, as she began to search for a Beat album. He looked as cheerful as the yellow daffodils on the campus front lawn. Then she laughed. Maybe Peter was only doing exactly what she was doing — ignoring Friday night, acting as though nothing had happened between them. She frowned. It seemed to be awfully easy for him.

Well, I'll show you, Peter Lacey, Monica resolved. This is one girl who's not going to waste any more time pining over you. She pulled out the albums he'd requested and marched back into the studio. This will be just as easy for me as it is for you.

"Here are your records, Peter," Monica said. Her voice was a lot sweeter now.

"Thanks, Monica. Put them right here." He pointed to the counter. "Uh, about the other night, I hope you're not too upset."

Monica was surprised, but she caught herself before it showed on her face.

"Upset? Why should I be? You did what you had to do." It took all her strength to force the words out.

"I'm glad," Peter said. "I really want you to help me with the show. I thought I'd do something a little different today — all British male singers. What do you think?"

"If I were grading you I'd give you a B plus."

"Not an A?"

"Nobody's perfect," she said.

Peter thumbed through the records. "Hey, Monica, you forgot a record. Where's Billy Idol?"

Monica feigned a gasp. "Oh, is that what that was? I couldn't read your scribble. I'll go get it. Be right back."

Peter watched her leave the room. His fingers rapped the counter again, this time in frustration. He still felt a thrill when Monica walked in. He thought the pink and blue dress she was wearing was adorable, and his first impulse was to get up, pick her up in his arms, and tell her he wanted to take up where they left off the other night. But he quickly checked himself. He had thought long and hard about it all weekend, and had come to the conclusion he could never do that to Lisa.

Peter had thought he would be glad Monica had decided to continue working at the station. But he hadn't anticipated the effect of Monica's presence on him, or the effect of Friday night on their working relationship. She was acting strictly professional. Their friendship was gone, along with their romance.

Monica came back in with the Billy Idol record. "Here it is — though why you want to play this stuff is beyond me."

"I'm not exactly a big fan either," Peter said. "But a lot of people out there like him. That's my job, to play what they want, not to amuse myself." This is ridiculous, he thought. I sound like a robot.

"I know that," Monica sniffed. "Here." She held out the album. Peter tried to take it from her, but missed. The record fell between them, and both stooped down to pick it up.

"I can get it," Monica said scoldingly.

Both their hands reached it simultaneously. For a brief instant they connected. Peter felt himself start to melt. When their fingers collided all the emotions came rushing back to him in one fell swoop.

Monica quickly stood up and turned her back to Peter. "You may have to play it, but I don't have to listen to it. I just remembered, I've got to study for a quiz next period. I've got to go down to the library right now."

"Yeah, sure," Peter said, waving a good-bye as she left. He turned the monitor up full blast, hoping it could drown out his thoughts.

Chapter 12

Monica bit into her cheeseburger as she continued her story. ". . . So I couldn't stand being in the same room with him. I had to get away. I just hope I feel better about this tomorrow."

"You will," said Kim, reaching for a French fry. "I'm so sorry this happened, Monica. In a way, I feel responsible, I should have seen it coming. Actually I did, but I thought you were going into it knowing the score."

The cheeseburger caught in Monica's throat. "You knew?"

"Hey, don't get mad at me. I tried to warn you, but you assured me you knew exactly what you were doing. Remember? You were so sure of Peter that if I'd come out and told you point blank about Lisa, you would have told me I didn't know what I was talking about. And don't try to deny it."

The cheeseburger felt like a lump in Monica's

stomach. She knew she shouldn't have eaten it, feeling as miserable as she did. But Kim had insisted she have something, especially since she hadn't eaten lunch. Kim was wrong about that, but Monica had to admit she was right about her attitude toward Peter. She wouldn't have believed anything Kim had told her before the date.

"So now what do I do?" Monica asked.

"Do what any other girl would do in this case. Find yourself another guy. Face it, Peter is taken. Why waste your time crying over him, when you can be having fun with someone else?"

"I don't want someone else."

"You can't have Peter."

"So I'll stay home alone."

"And be miserable? What kind of fun is that?"

"You don't stop loving someone just like that." She snapped her fingers.

"I'm not saying you have to fall in love with the next guy you date. But you can go out and have a good time. How do you know you wouldn't? It's not like you've gone out with hundreds of boys before Peter."

"I know what you're trying to say. I'm very inexperienced with boys, and I feel so strongly about Peter because he's the first decent boy who ever showed interest in me. But that's not true." She touched her heart. "I know it in here."

Kim glanced at Monica's cheeseburger. "Are you going to finish that?" When Monica shook her head, Kim reached over and picked it up. Before taking a bite she said, "Everything you just told me may be true, but it's irrelevant. You can't live on a one-way relationship. You need to be out there circulating."

"Great," Monica said sarcastically. "So what do I do — point to the next guy who walks by and say. 'You're going out with me'?"

"No, you let me fix you up on a blind date."

Monica winced. "That's gross."

"Only if the guy's a real nerdbrain. What if I can get you a date with a nice guy?"

"Who?"

Kim tapped her index finger thoughtfully on her mouth. "I'm not sure yet. I'm going to give Woody a call, and check something out." She put down the remnants of the cheeseburger. "I'll be right back. Don't you move."

Monica sipped her soda as she pondered the possibilities. She was interrupted a moment later by the arrival of Phoebe, Chris, Sasha, and Ted. "Mind if we crash your booth?" Chris asked.

"Join the party," Monica said. She was grateful for the company. At least now Kim wouldn't bug her about her love life.

Ted slid into the booth opposite Monica. Chris and Phoebe followed, as Sasha moved into the space next to Monica.

"Congratulations, Monica," Phoebe said. The others joined in.

Monica looked at them like they were aliens. She hadn't done anything worth celebrating. "I'm sorry, I don't know what you're talking about," she admitted.

"The radio show," Sasha said.

"That's old news. I've been helping Peter out for the past two weeks," she explained.

"No," Sasha continued. "We mean the show you're doing on Friday."

"How'd you find out about it?"

"The whole school knows, Monica," Chris said. "Peter announced it at the end of his show today. Weren't you listening?"

"N-no," she admitted. "I left early. He really said it?"

"You sound surprised," Chris said. "Hadn't he told you?"

"Yes. But I didn't know he still meant it." Lest she raise suspicions she added quickly, "You know how possessive he is about the show. I thought he may have offered me it in a moment of weakness. I'm glad he still wants me to do it."

"You don't know how lucky you are," Sasha said, digging into the grapefruit she'd brought with her. "Peter told me you were doing a great job, but none of his assistants has ever gone on the air. How'd you manage it?"

"I auditioned for him last week," she answered.

"What are you going to do?" Sasha wondered.

"I don't know yet," Monica said, brightening. "But I guarantee it'll be a half hour to remember."

"I know one thing you're going to do," Phoebe interjected. "You're going to come over to my house Friday night for a celebration party."

"I'm afraid she can't," Kim said, having just returned from the pay phone. "Monica's got a date."

"Then we'll make it Saturday." Phoebe shrugged. "It'll give me an extra day to recover from my trip." Turning to Monica she asked, "Who are you going out with?"

Kim quickly spoke up. "Just one of the most sought-after guys in Silver Spring — Carter Smith." She smiled smugly at Monica as if to say: There's no getting out of it now!

Chapter
13

The taxi stopped at the corner of Broadway and Forty-third Street. "We're here, Miss," the driver said.

Phoebe paid the man and tried to open the door. It wouldn't budge. "It's locked," he said.

She looked at the large metal bolt on the door. It didn't look like any car lock she'd ever seen before. But New York was unlike any city she'd ever been in before, and she'd arrived only the night before. She finally managed to unlock the door. "Thanks a lot," she said to the driver, as she slammed the door closed. But he was already off chasing another passenger before the words were out of her mouth. Phoebe wondered if she'd ever figure out the secret to catching a cab in New York. She'd stood outside the hotel for ten minutes trying to flag one down, but had no luck until Mrs. Webster came down and got one for her. She'd never had to do this before. She had always gotten around Washington by bus or subway, and the only kinds of taxis she'd ever been in were the kind her father called by phone to take the family to the airport.

Phoebe stretched her neck, looking up at the skyscrapers surrounding her. They were much taller than the office buildings in Washington, and they had a different feel to them. They were shoved together on the island of Manhattan like crayons stacked in a box.

Phoebe was glad she'd remembered to pack a sweater. It had been warm when she left Washington on the train with Woody's mother, but Griffin had told her to be prepared for anything. So when she woke up and saw the cloudy sky, she dug into her suitcase and took out the sweater. It was one of her favorites, a bulky, olive-green cable-knit pullover. A pair of stonewashed jeans over a pair of leather boots completed her outfit.

The sky was still overcast, scribbled with gray. Phoebe hoped it didn't mean rain. But even a thunderstorm wouldn't have soured her mood. She was in New York, just moments away from her reunion with Griffin.

Phoebe checked the paper in her jeans pocket, then looked again at the address on the granite-faced building in front of her. She had the right place, but none of the scores of people who passed her by looked like Griffin.

Phoebe began to pace around the entrance of the building, both to keep warm, and to have something to do. She looked down at her watch. It was five after nine. Griffin wasn't really late, but she had hoped he'd be so excited to see her that he'd have come early.

She spotted a street cart near the curb and remembered she hadn't eaten breakfast. An old, bent man was selling pretzels, and Phoebe felt so sorry for him she bought two even though she wasn't that hungry.

When she turned around she saw a moderately tall boy propped up against the side of the building. Griffin. He was wearing jeans, a baggy gray wool blazer, and a long black scarf around his neck. It wasn't the most fashionable outfit, but Phoebe thought there was something about his nonchalant pose that made him stand out in the crowd.

Phoebe's heart raced. Seeing Griffin made her realize how much she'd missed him, and how much lost time they had to make up for in the short while they'd be together. She called out to him as she approached, "Hey, there, could I offer a pretzel to a young struggling actor?"

"Phoebe!" Griffin's face opened into the widest smile Phoebe had seen in months.

Phoebe raced toward Griffin and fell into his arms. Even though she was in a strange city, she'd felt as if she'd just come home. Griffin was even wearing the same after-shave, the light, slightly musky scent that fit him so perfectly. Phoebe wished she hadn't bought the pretzels so she'd have her hands free to hug him the way she'd like.

Phoebe let herself relax and enjoy the wonderful sensation of Griffin's arms around her. When she opened her eyes to look at him, she realized the sun had peeked out from behind the clouds and was beaming down upon them.

"You look terrific, Phoebe," Griffin told her. "Thanks for getting me my breakfast, too." He took a bite of the still-warm pretzel. "Sorry I'm late. The double R broke down again."

The double *what*? she wanted to ask. But not wanting to appear ignorant of city life, she said nothing, and bit into her pretzel.

Griffin continued, "I knew I should have walked, but I got up late and the train is faster. . . ."

Phoebe stuck another piece of pretzel in his mouth. "It doesn't matter. The important thing is that we're together. And we won't have much time. So let's make the most of it."

Griffin swallowed hard. "See these?" He indicated a wad of papers in his blazer pocket. "I've got to run them up to some producers in this building first."

"May I help?"

"Of course." He took one out to show her. "Fliers for the play. All of us have been taking these around to agents and producers all over town."

"Haven't any of them come to see it?"

"Not as many as we'd like." He sighed. "I guess they don't come unless you really push. There are a lot of showcases going on all the time."

"I can't wait to see it," Phoebe said.

"I can," Griffin said.

Phoebe fretted her brow. "Problems?"

He patted her back. "No. I just want to make

the hours before the play stretch as long as possible." He offered her his arm. "Let's get this out of the way. Then the day is all ours."

Phoebe and Griffin raced through the black-and-white-tiled halls of the office building. They dropped off fliers at nearly every office, even at the non-theatrical businesses. "If they're in this building, they must like the theater," Griffin reasoned.

A half hour later they were back on the street. Phoebe noticed that the theater lights, as well as the advertising billboards that surrounded Times Square, remained lit during the day. She kept that observation to herself, thinking Griffin would find nothing noteworthy about that.

Holding hands, they began to walk down Broadway. They hadn't gone far when Griffin steered her into a small storefront. He grabbed a small plastic object and handed it to the cashier along with a few dollars. He moved too fast for Phoebe to see what he'd bought.

He handed her the bag when they got outside. "My present to you. A little souvenir from the Big Apple."

"Oh, Griffin, you didn't have to do that. Souvenirs are for tourists." Griffin's mouth tightened into a frown. "I'm sorry, Griffin," she apologized immediately. "I just meant, you don't have a lot of money. You don't have to buy me things."

"What if I want to?" he asked.

Phoebe smiled. "Then I'll take it gladly." She ripped open the brown bag. Inside was a plastic ball with a big theater marquee that said "Broadway." Phoebe shook it and watched with glee as

120

the snow began to fall over it. "It's great. I like it," she said, planting a kiss on his cheek. "I've got a surprise for you, too."

"What is it?"

"If I told you, it'd spoil the surprise. I'm saving it for later." She shook the plastic ball again. "I've got the perfect place for this — right on my bookcase, next to the picture I'm going to take of you." She opened the flap of her leather carryall and took out a camera. "Did you know I don't have any?"

He nodded. "I don't have any of you, either," he said as they continued walking. "I haven't needed them. I keep a picture of you here all the time." He pointed to his head.

"I'm afraid my memory's not as sharp as yours."

"I'd be happy to pose for you, madam," he said. "But not here on Broadway, at least not till I've landed my first real role."

"How about Central Park then?" she asked. "There are some pretty spots off of Seventy-second Street, near the lake."

He nodded. "You really do know the city, don't you?"

"I told you I did. My dad used to take me up here a lot when I was younger." The lie slipped easily from her tongue, and Griffin didn't notice.

"Maybe we'll even take a boat ride later." He looked questioningly at the sky. "That is, if it doesn't rain. Right now I thought we'd continue down Broadway and take a nice leisurely walk to SoHo."

Phoebe remembered from her map study that

SoHo was miles away. "We're going to walk all that way?"

Griffin shrugged. "That's the great thing about New York. You can go for miles and hardly realize it. There's so much to see."

When they neared Thirty-fourth Street, Griffin asked Phoebe if she wanted to go up to the top of the Empire State Building. Phoebe scoffed as she looked upward. The top of the building was obscured by the low clouds that had returned to the sky. She'd never been in any building that high and would have loved to go, but she declined his offer. "I've been," she lied easily. "Once you've done it, it's no big deal."

"Whatever," Griffin said.

Around Eighteenth Street, Phoebe realized her feet had begun to swell. She cursed herself for wearing the boots. They were made to look good, not to withstand the pounding of the Manhattan pavement. She could feel every pebble through the thin soles, and wondered if anything remained of the tiny stiletto heel. By Fourteenth Street her pace had slowed considerably, and she began to lag behind Griffin's still spritely step.

He turned around and called playfully, "Hey, slowpoke, what are you doing?"

Phoebe jogged to catch up with Griffin. "I just remembered something. There's a really good art show at a gallery I know of in SoHo."

"I didn't know you were into art," Griffin said. "If I'd known, we could have headed in the other direction. There's a fantastic show at the Whitney."

"Oh, I've been there," she said, although she'd

never heard of it before. "They have some wonderful pieces. Maybe we'll go the next time I come to town." It wasn't just the lying that was making it hard for her to get the words out. Her feet felt as if they were being squeezed by twin vises. Yet she walked on, pretending nothing was wrong. By her calculations they were within striking distance of SoHo. They were running out of streets with numbers; soon they'd be coming to the streets with names.

Griffin pointed off to the right as they approached Eighth Street. "NYU is over there," he said. "That's one school you might consider applying to. It's got a good all-around program, and something a lot of other schools can't give you."

"What's that?"

"Me. If you went there, we could be together a lot more often. Of course that's more than a year away, but it's never too early to start thinking."

"S-sure," Phoebe said, wincing.

Griffin turned around. "Did I say something wrong?"

Phoebe's toes were beginning to feel numb. "Griffin, there's something I've got to tell you. You're going to have to carry me to SoHo. My feet have died." She explained about her boots.

"You picked a good time to complain," he told her. "There's a shoe store right across the street."

Phoebe gratefully hobbled inside, and traded her boots for a pair of white leather sneakers. They cost her nearly all her spending money, but it was worth it. When she rejoined Griffin outside she felt more like a human being again. "How dumb of me," she told him. "I should have known better."

He shook his head. "You're not used to walking. It's not the sort of thing you think about in Rose Hill," he told her.

"Do you miss it?"

"Except for you, no," he said. "There's nothing else worth going back for. Everything I want is here."

Taking Phoebe's hand, Griffin pranced to the window of an antiques store. "Have you ever seen anything like that in your life?"

He pointed to a large, wood-framed, upholstered sofa that had to be at least twelve feet long and four feet tall. The cloth was hand painted, with a medieval-looking portrait of cherubs sitting in a field of grass and wildflowers. The mahogany frame was intricately carved with a series of suns and dragons. "It's really unusual," Phoebe agreed. It was the ugliest piece of furniture she'd ever seen.

They continued hand-in-hand until they reached a street whose name Phoebe recognized, the street where the gallery was located. It was just a few buildings down from Broadway so Phoebe was able to point it out to Griffin as if it were an old familiar landmark. Confidently she led him into the building. "You're going to love this," she told him.

Phoebe spoke prematurely. Monica had told her it was a modern art show, but she hadn't told her how modern. The paintings were cartoons of nude men and women in bright, unnatural colors. They were awful, she thought. Monica had said they were good.

Phoebe snickered to herself. Monica must have told her to impress her, just as she was trying to impress Griffin.

After the fifth painting, Phoebe whispered, "I've had enough of these."

Griffin smiled. "I'm glad you said that. I was worried you actually liked this stuff."

Phoebe searched for a way to recover from her embarrassment. "Well, I've seen some of this artist's other work, and believe me, it's nothing like this. They were landscapes."

After lunch in SoHo, Griffin took Phoebe on the subway back up to Central Park. She took out her camera and shot an entire roll of pictures of Griffin. He wouldn't sit still for a pose, but insisted she shoot candids of him in various locations. She shot him trying to climb a stone fence, talking to the balloon man outside the children's zoo, and even hanging upside down on monkey bars.

Phoebe's heart once again filled with love for this unusual boy. She'd never known anyone who had so much boundless enthusiasm, who was always ready for a new adventure or challenge. She was surprised when he led her to the boats and insisted on taking her out on the lake. The sky had darkened considerably, and Phoebe was starting to feel a chill under her sweater. She didn't want to admit it, but all their running around had tired her. Even in her new sneakers, her feet were getting sore again.

"It'll be much calmer on the water," he told her. "Besides, there's no one else out there, and I've been dying to be alone with you all day."

"Couldn't we go back to your place?" she wondered.

"You wouldn't like it," he said. "And one of my roommates works nights, so he's sleeping there now. We wouldn't be alone."

Phoebe saw the twinkle in his bright eyes, and she had to say yes to the boat ride. She could be adventurous, too. And in the boat she'd be able to sit down and rest her feet. "But you have to let me row," she insisted. "You've got to rest up for the play."

He shrugged. "That's hours away."

He helped her set the boat in the water. Slowly, they drifted out onto the murky lake. They were the only ones out. "Alone at last," he whispered. "Anyone for a round of 'Row, Row, Row Your Boat'?"

"I think you just did it." Instead of rowing, Phoebe lifted the oars out of the water and placed them inside the boat. She was content to let the boat drift where it might. "It's hard to believe we're in the middle of the city," she noted, resting her head on the boat's stern. On the water's edge were an old man and a young girl, grandfather and granddaughter, perhaps, flying a red and white kite in the rising breezes. Except for the upper stories of the apartment buildings in the distance, Phoebe might have thought she was in

Rose Hill. In the silence, they heard the rumble of thunder far off.

"I like to come here when I need to think," Griffin said. He was lying down on the opposite side of the boat, his feet toe to toe with Phoebe's. "Sometimes being out there can be very frustrating."

"I've wondered about that — all those months you were pounding the streets after that Broadway role fell through. You've never told me what it was really like."

"I'd still rather not."

"Don't you trust me?"

"Of course — "

"Well, why won't you talk to me about it?"

"It's not that I'm trying to hide anything. . . . It's just something I'd rather forget."

Phoebe heard an intense sadness in his voice, and didn't push him any further. "I understand."

"No, Phoebe, you really don't. Believe me, you don't want to, and I don't want you to ever have to experience anything like it. Months of rejection can make you lose sense of yourself."

"And lose sense of those who really care about you," Phoebe finished.

Griffin looked at Phoebe. The intensity of his love was spread across his face. It was that intensity, that passion for every moment, that Phoebe loved most about him. "Is that your way of saying you still want me?" he asked.

Phoebe glanced up at the sky. Dark clouds were moving in from the northwest. A small flock of geese was flying away, to shelter, Phoebe hoped. The man and the girl had drawn in their kite and had headed for home. She looked back at Griffin. "It's chilly over here," she said.

"I'm coming." Griffin gingerly maneuvered himself to Phoebe's side of the boat. They had drifted toward the center of the lake, close to a small, barren island. He lowered his long, thin legs under the center seats, and slunk down until his head was just above Phoebe's.

He lifed her into his arms. "I love you, Phoebe," he said as he gently placed his lips on hers.

Phoebe responded eagerly to Griffin's kiss. She ran her fingers through his hair. She wiped thoughts of anyone else from her mind. She was with Griffin and would have been content to stay right where she was forever.

A drop of water woke her from her reverie. It was followed by another, and a moment later Griffin eased over and turned his head upward. A bright-pink vein of lightning shattered the dark sky, and the bellow of thunder that accompanied it was loud enough to make even Griffin shudder. "I'll row," he shouted, having to raise his voice to be heard above the thunder, and the sheets of rain.

Phoebe looked at the nearby island. "Maybe we should stay here," she called.

Even soaked to the bone, Griffin managed a smile. "We can't — I've got a show to do to-night."

A few minutes later they were back on shore, a little safer, but no drier. They ducked into the boathouse to get out of the rain. Phoebe bought two cups of hot chocolate. The man at the counter looked at her as if she had been crazy to have

128

rented the boat in the first place. "I'd always heard it was dangerous to be out on the water during a lightning storm," she told Griffin. "Sudden death, or something almost as gruesome. We could have died out there."

"But we didn't." Griffin put an arm around her as they watched the storm through a floor-to-ceiling window. "You're with me, Pheeb. And nothing's going to happen when I'm around."

Griffin's hair had plastered itself to his forehead. It looked a little like a helmet, and the image made Phoebe giggle. "Your friends are going to wonder when you walk in looking like this," she said.

He rubbed his hand on her own unkempt hair. "Pheeb, we're both a mess. We'd better get cleaned up right now."

Chapter 14

Phoebe thought if her mother could have seen her, she would have killed her.

She was sitting on a well-worn sofa in Griffin's living room, wrapped in his blue terry cloth robe. Her jeans were drying on the old-fashioned radiator under the window, her sweater hanging from the shower curtain rod in the tiny bathroom.

Phoebe wasn't sure she'd argue with her mother. Griffin's apartment was as dismal as he had promised. Like everything else she'd encountered in New York so far, it was very different from what she expected.

She looked around the small rectangular room, waiting for Griffin to finish dressing in the bathroom. In one corner was a mattress where Griffin's roommate had been sleeping until they arrived. He scampered off quickly soon after they got there, leaving them alone. The only other pieces of furniture in the room were a beat-up coffee table, an armchair that looked like a Salvation Army reject, and the sofa she was sitting on. It had more lumps than oatmeal, and she had discovered at least one broken spring, but even with those faults it was preferable to the chair.

How could Griffin, with his sensitivity and artistic nature, stand living like this? she wondered. Phoebe wasn't just being a snob about the furniture. She knew Griffin was struggling to make a living. But the place was a mess. Clothes were strewn over the floor, along with empty envelopes from the previous day's mail. A few newspapers were stacked haphazardly in one corner. And there were no touches that transformed the place from an anonymous apartment into a home. Where Phoebe had imagined bright theater posters were naked walls; on the table where she had imagined framed photographs stood dirty, dried-out tumblers.

Griffin emerged from the bathroom, carrying something in his hand. "Here, try this on." He opened up his arms to reveal a big blue-and-white striped shirt. "It's the best I can offer."

Phoebe got up and took the shirt. "It beats a wet anything, I suppose." She retreated to the bathroom and came out wearing the shirt. On her body, it fit like a dress, and with the sleeves rolled up it was surprisingly fashionable. All she needed was a belt and her boots, which had escaped the drenching, and her outfit would be complete. "If you decide to give up acting, you can always go into the dress designing business. This is genius," she told him.

"I wouldn't go that far, but it looks a lot better

on you than it ever did on me." Griffin kissed her
on the cheek. "I don't know if I told you, but
I'm going out with some of the cast after the
show. I'd like you to come along, if you can.
What time do you have to be back at the hotel?"

"Midnight."

"We'll have plenty of time, then. I'd like you
to meet some of the gang. There's this one guy,
Barney, who's really terrific. When he was our
age he made his living catching pies in the face
on the carnival circuit. He must be around fifty
now, and I can stay up all night listening to his
stories."

"I can't wait," Phoebe said, sighing. Anything
to get out of this creepy dump, she thought, as a
bug unlike any she had ever seen in Rose Hill
scuttled up the wall next to Griffin.

Griffin placed his hands on Phoebe's shoulders. "Now how about that surprise you promised me?"

She gasped. "I forgot all about it." She reached
for her carryall on the coffee table and dug out
the tape of her radio performance. She handed
it to Griffin. "My radio debut." In answer to his
astonished stare she continued, "Peter asked me
to sing on his show last week. He made a tape
of it, and I want you to have it."

"Terrific." Griffin went to the bedroom and
flicked it into his cassette deck. "I'm going to
play it right now."

"I'm anxious to know what you think."

"I'm sure I'm going to love it. You've got a
great voice."

"No, I mean, what you really think. Like

132

you're hearing someone you never met. I want you to be brutally honest."

Griffin shrugged. "Okay, if you insist." He pressed the play button and closed his eyes as he listed to Phoebe sing. Phoebe tried to read his expression. His face was maddeningly blank, his look a far cry from the rapturous one he wore the day they sang together at the Follies.

As soon as the song was over he turned off the machine. "That was nice," he said.

Phoebe smiled. It was a good start. It meant a lot that Griffin still thought she had a lovely voice. "Go on," she said.

"You really want to know what I think?" he asked. His voice was gentle, but there was an undertone that made Phoebe nervous. Phoebe was no longer sure brutal honesty was what she wanted. Since Griffin had been in New York, he had had lots of opportunities to sing with real professionals. Phoebe knew she was talented, but she hadn't had any training. She couldn't hope to compare favorably to the people he'd been with recently. But she didn't want Griffin to think she couldn't handle professional criticism. "Yes," she answered.

"Your voice is as strong as it was when we sang in the Follies. You've got a lot of potential, but your phrasing is off. You're not selling the message of the song. You're singing the words, but it's hard to believe you mean them."

Phoebe's stomach began to contract. She had sung her heart out thinking of Griffin that day, and it was Griffin who was tearing her to pieces. "But I did," she said. She was trying to keep her tone light and carefree, but her voice vibrated with tension.

"It's nothing that a good vocal coach can't fix," Griffin continued. "But you're not ready for the pros yet, if that's what you want to know. You've got a lot of work ahead of you."

Phoebe waved her arms in the air in frustration. One of the sleeves started to unfold, flopping over her hand. "I shouldn't have brought it," she said. "I wanted you to like it."

Griffin rose and started to move close. "I didn't say I didn't. But you wanted me to be honest with you, and I was." He reached out to take her in his arms, but she edged away from him.

Phoebe felt confused. She no longer knew why she had wanted Griffin to be so critical. She should have known he couldn't be anything but honest with her. And she already knew her untrained voice was full of imperfections.

"You were right, Griffin. I'm sorry I overreacted. I guess I'm just frazzled from the day. I think I need a cup of tea."

Phoebe walked to the kitchen. She flicked on the light in the postage-stamp-sized cubbyhole that passed for a kitchen. "Auggggghhhh!"

Griffin rushed to her side. "What's wrong?"

She pointed to the army of cockroaches crawling along the cracked linoleum. "Make them go away," she said.

"Can't," he said casually. "We've tried killing them, but they always come back." He moved her aside to get into the kitchen, then filled the copper teakettle on the stovetop with water.

"What kind of tea would you like, herbal or regular?"

Phoebe's stomach lurched. "How can you stand this?" she exclaimed, holding out her hands. "Those roaches are everywhere."

"They're a fact of New York City life. Even the best apartments get them."

"But they're so dirty. And this place." She looked around, her upper lip curled in disgust. "Oh, Griffin, why do you live this way?"

"I don't really have a choice," he told her. "This is just surface stuff, appearances. What really counts is what this city has to offer me: an opportunity to learn my craft and really make it as an actor. I can never lose sight of that."

"But it's awful, Griffin. It gives me the creeps being here."

Phoebe couldn't meet Griffin's gaze. She had said the words she tried to keep to herself since she'd arrived. Griffin's silence told her she had made a big mistake.

"It's my life," he said finally, an air of defiance creeping into his voice. "I may have to live like this for a long time, till I make it as an actor."

"Isn't there another way?"

"I wish there were. Between working my day job, doing the play, and taking acting classes, I barely have time to sleep. And somewhere in all that I have to squeeze in the time to study for my high school equivalency. I haven't had a day off like this in months. But even with all that, I'm not complaining. Getting up on that stage before a live audience makes it all worthwhile. It's a sacrifice I can deal with. Can you?"

"I don't know," she admitted. "It all made sense back in Rose Hill, but here it's all so different. The strange streets, the strange people, the strange food. I've never seen anything like it before."

"I thought you knew New York."

She shook her head. "I've never been here before. I lied to you about that. I wanted you to think I belonged in this city, so I read up on everything so I could pretend I knew my way around like a native. But I messed it all up. I don't know anything about art galleries. I don't know anything about Central Park. I don't know anything about cockroaches — and I don't want to." Sadly she picked up her carryall and marched to the door. "I never should have come here. We were perfect together in Rose Hill, but I could never make it here. I'm sure that's ten times as clear to you as it is to me."

"Phoebe, wait — " Griffin called as Phoebe ran out the door and down the four flights of steps to the first floor. As much as she wanted him to catch up with her, Phoebe continued to run. She had struggled to make sure everything about her visit with Griffin was perfect. But her efforts had only helped to ruin the day. Added to the strain of the disaster at the art gallery, and her aching feet, Griffin's comments about her song and his dismal apartment were more than she could bear. Breathing heavily, Phoebe collapsed against the pole of a traffic signal. When she looked back, Griffin was gone, the front door of his building shut. Wincing at the pain of her throbbing feet, Phoebe limped on.

Chapter
15

As she walked through Greenwich Village, Phoebe wiped away the tears that stung her face. Slowly, the cool night air helped bring her to her senses. A few blocks later, she realized she had overreacted terribly. It was the result of a day spent living a lie. She never should have tried to impress Griffin by pretending to know more about the city than she really did know. In Rose Hill it had made sense to her, but all she had ended up doing was making herself look like a fool.

Phoebe wanted to apologize to Griffin and start all over again. She didn't mean half the things she had told him. She was proud of the way he'd been able to carve out a life for himself in this city. It wasn't the way she'd want to live, but it wasn't her life. And all the things that upset her were just surface matters; she still loved Griffin very much.

There was a pizza stand on the corner, and Phoebe bought two slices as a peace offering to bring back to his apartment. But when she rang the buzzer next to his name at the front door, no one responded. Phoebe realized she had lost all track of time, but it was beginning to get dark. She concluded Griffin must have left for his show. Sitting at the top of the stoop, she ate both slices of pizza. Feeling full and a lot more in control of herself, Phoebe checked the address that Griffin had given her and went in search of the theater.

The theater was just a few blocks away, on the ground floor of what once had been a factory building. The bright cloth banners that hung outside the entrance were the only drops of color on the otherwise gray street. Phoebe joined the small line of ticket buyers waiting for the doors to open. She wrapped herself in her arms, trying hard to stay warm. The thin cotton shirt barely protected her from the cool, damp night air. She unrolled the sleeves and wrapped them around her hands. At least it had stopped raining. Finally, the doors opened and the line began to move.

The play was a comedy about an office computer that went haywire. Griffin played the meek office boy who tamed the computer and saved the company. Phoebe couldn't deny that his skills had grown since the days of the Kennedy High Follies. After the cast took its second curtain call and the houselights went up, she got directions from the nearest usher and made her way backstage.

Griffin was nowhere to be seen. An actress told Phoebe she thought Griffin had run out as soon as he got offstage. She didn't know where he had gone.

Phoebe was crushed. She had stared straight at him the entire time he was on stage. He had looked straight at her several times. The theater was so small, he had to have known she was there.

Dazed and tired, Phoebe drifted out of the theater, a new round of tears mixing with the rain that had started falling again. She was able to get a cab to the hotel right away. Phoebe wondered if it was pure luck, or whether the sight of a crying girl with matted red hair, an oversized shirt, and no jacket evoked sympathy from the cab driver. As the cab sped uptown, however, she realized she wasn't ready to face Mrs. Webster, and have to tell her what a disaster her day had become. She told the driver to pull up in front of a movie theater. Before she could change her mind, she bought a ticket and went inside to watch the second half of a movie she realized she had already seen.

It was close to midnight by the time Phoebe returned to the hotel room. Mrs. Webster was sitting in a chair waiting for her. There was a brown paper bag near her feet. "Where have you been?" she demanded. Mrs. Webster had that mixed look of anger and worry Phoebe knew so well from her own mother.

Phoebe couldn't lie to her. "Oh, Mrs. Webster, it was so awful." Her eyes began to tear again.

"I can see. What are you doing dressed like that?"

"It's a long story."

Woody's mother reached out her arms, and Phoebe flew into them willingly. "Tell me about it, dear," Mrs. Webster prodded gently.

Phoebe poured out her story, finally explaining why she was running around on a cool New York night in a boy's shirt. "I never should have run out on him. He must hate me. Now I'm never going to see him again," she said, sobbing. "How could I have been so stupid? This was supposed to be one of the happiest days of my life, but I've gone and blown it." Phoebe got up and went to the bathroom for a tissue.

"Maybe, maybe not, Phoebe," Mrs. Webster said slyly.

Curious, Phoebe returned to the room. "What do you mean?" she asked. She fell onto one of the double beds.

"Griffin was here. He wanted you to have this." She pointed to the bag.

Phoebe picked it up. Inside were her sweater, jeans, and sneakers. "When was this?"

"He said he'd come from the theater. He waited about an hour, then he left. He said he would call you this weekend."

"Did he say anything else?"

"Only that you had some kind of misunderstanding. But I think you're going to be able to work it out," Mrs. Webster said.

Phoebe wasn't so sure. "I wouldn't blame him if he came here to tell me he didn't want to see me again," she told Mrs. Webster, as she dabbed her eyes with another tissue. "A lot of things have changed since we were together in Rose Hill.

Living here on his own has made him grow up. He's got a lot of responsibilities, and his life is anything but easy. I'm still a high school junior — a kid. A point I made abundantly clear tonight."

Mrs. Webster patted her hand. "He seemed to care for you, Phoebe. Don't go jumping to conclusions."

"You don't know Griffin. He probably put on a happy face for your benefit. But it's not that I think he doesn't care about me. It's — it's . . ." She let out a sigh. "I'm afraid we're growing in different directions."

Mrs. Webster rose from the bed and began pacing around the room. "You know, Phoebe, you never asked me why I agreed to let you come here with me — "

"I've ruined your trip," Phoebe blurted out.

Mrs. Webster slowly shook her head. Then she reached out and gently touched Phoebe's hand. "Let me go on," she said. "When I first heard about your plans, it brought back a lot of memories for me. You see, long before I met Woody's dad I was in love with an actor, too."

"You were?" Phoebe said, amazed.

"Yes. I was living here, and had just gotten my first role in an off-Broadway play. He was acting in a show on Broadway. He was tall, handsome, broad-shouldered, with a mane of dark hair. There was something special about him. He was commanding and powerful, but at the same time gentle and sensitive. Anyway, every night we used to meet in Shubert Alley after our shows. We did a lot of silly things that young people in love always do." Phoebe thought she saw a new twinkle in Mrs. Webster's eyes, as she watched her live the memory. "One particular night he told me to meet him at a very famous restaurant called Sardi's, where all the actors who had already become successful used to meet. I waited and waited outside for hours, but he never showed up."

"Why?"

"He called me the next day — from California. He had been rushed out there on very short notice to do a movie. He promised he would come back, but the roles kept coming, and he couldn't abandon his dream."

Phoebe thought she saw the trace of a tear in Mrs. Webster's eyes. "What did you do?"

"I didn't let it crush me," she said. "I had the memories of all the wonderful times we had. No one could take them away from me. He touched my heart in a very special way, and even to this day I still have good feelings about the time we shared."

"Do you ever wonder what happened to him?"

"He became a very famous movie actor."

"Who is he?" Phoebe wondered.

"It's not important, but the reason I told you is. Life is a continuing series of moments, adventures, and encounters, to be discovered and savored. If things between you and Griffin work out, that'll be great. But if they don't, there's a whole world waiting for you." She ambled over to the window and looked out at the still active cityscape below. She snapped her fingers. "It's your last night in New York City. This is one of the most exciting places in the world, and you barely got to scratch the surface today. Let's go somewhere and celebrate being alive."

"But where will we go this time of night?"

Mrs. Webster smiled. "How about Sardi's?"

In a flash, Phoebe saw an image of the young Mrs. Webster running happily into the famous restaurant. Maybe a night on the town wouldn't be so bad, after all. "Okay," she smiled. "Just as soon as I change my clothes."

Chapter
16

"This is Monica Ford, bringing you all the hits on WKND, the voice of Kennedy High. Now here's an oldie-but-goodie from Phil Collins."

Monica turned off her mike and turned up the record. This time it wasn't practice. She shivered as a cold chill ran down her spine. Now everyone at Kennedy knew who she was. She really was on the air!

She had not expected to feel the way she did — like a locomotive running in high gear. She wasn't doing anything she hadn't practiced over and over again all that week. The mechanical moves she made were the same. Yet there was an urgency in her movements now, a keen sense that the clock was running. And she was under pressure to keep an eye on everything: the record now playing, the one she was about to cue up, and the stack awaiting her on the counter, not to mention the mike, monitors, and dials.

When she had practiced, the tasks flowed smoothly, one into the next. Now that she was actually doing the show, her nerves started to overwhelm her. Suddenly, there seemed to be an uncountable number of things to do.

The Phil Collins number was almost over, so Monica flipped open her mike, ready to introduce the next record. Taking a deep breath she sighed, then realized that the noise could be heard over the air. She quickly faded the music down and spoke. "That was Phil Collins. Now, let's rock, with a classic cut from the historic Live Aid concert."

She pressed the button to start the turntable, but the monitor remained silent. She turned around. The turntable was spinning, and the needle was on the record. She didn't understand what was wrong. But she knew she'd committed the worst sin of radio: dead air.

Monica knew she couldn't panic. She opened her mike again. "There seems to be a bug in the old turntable," she said, surprised she could get the words out. She had to think fast. "It's holding our Live Aid cut hostage. While we figure out how to free it, let me tell you about the concert scene in the D.C. area this weekend. . . ." Quickly, she picked up the sheet of paper she had prepared to read later in the program.

As Monica read the list, her thoughts settled and she realized why the monitor wouldn't operate. She had forgotten to open the switch that fed the turntable signal to the transmitter. Her frantic heartbeat slowed down a little. Peter, who had stayed clear of the studio so far, was on his

way in from the record library, obviously determined to help her out. But she would be able to
tell him he wasn't needed. This problem was one
she could solve. Continuing to read, she rescued
the record, and opened up the switch. ". . . . Well,
we've managed to ransom that record. Now back
to the music."

She pressed the button again, cut her mike,
then slumped against the counter and sighed.

"It's not as easy as it looks, is it?" Peter
commented.

She looked up. "I'm doing okay," she told him
defiantly.

He took a step backward. "Hey, I didn't say
you weren't. I came in here to congratulate you
for thinking on your feet."

Monica shook her head. She and Peter had
hardly spoken to each other all week, going about
their work like robots. Monica found the only
way she could bear being in the same room with
Peter was to pretend she had no feelings for him
whatsoever. She knew Peter spoke sincerely, but
his compliment was more painful to her than
their neutral silence had been. "Thanks," she
answered. "For a moment there I panicked."

"But you recovered, and that's the important
thing. I guarantee you won't make that mistake
again."

She turned to the control board. "I can't talk.
I've got to get the next record up," she told him.
"How do you manage to be so relaxed?"

"Experience," he said. "I was just as frantic
as you the first time I did a show. I think I even
lost my voice."

146

"Don't say that!" she cried. "You'll give me ideas."

He patted her shoulder. "Relax, you're doing fine." He walked out of the studio to the library.

Peter's friendly touch was even more unbearable to Monica than the praise. It brought back the memories of touches that had held the promise of something more meaningful. Monica found it difficult to relax, with Peter now intruding upon her thoughts.

Monica had no choice but to force it out of her consciousness. She segued into a Racers tune, then ended the program with a medley of tunes by female vocalists. "And that'll do it for a Friday afternoon. This is Monica Ford wishing everybody a happy weekend. Tune in on Monday for the return of Peter Lacey. This is WKND, Rose Hill. The voice of Kennedy High."

She felt triumphant as she flicked the switch for the final time. Except for the minor blunder in the middle, she'd finished the show without falling to pieces. She felt like screaming Hooray! at the top of her lungs. But she settled for leaning back on the stool with a sigh of relief.

Peter was grinning broadly when he popped into the studio. "Well, you did it. Congratulations."

"I'm exhausted," she said, taking off the headphones. "Totally drained."

"You'll recover quickly. Do you think you'll want to give it another try next Friday?"

Monica stared at him openmouthed. "Do you really mean it?"

"You ought to know me well enough to realize I don't make offers like that to just anyone."

"Peter. I don't know what to say!"

"How about yes?" He gave her a boyish grin that stung her again. Even the best news, coming from Peter, couldn't entirely erase the pain of his nearness.

"Listen," he continued, "there's something else I wanted to tell you . . . before anyone else gets the word. Lisa's coming home tonight."

Monica felt as if she'd been slapped in the face. Her gratitude instantly became indignation. "What are you trying to do, bribe me, so I won't feel bad about you dragging your honey around town?"

"N-no," Peter said. "These things have nothing to do with each other — "

"Well, don't bother, Peter," Monica went on. "You can spend the entire weekend with Lisa, as far as I'm concerned. I'm going to be out with my new boyfriend tonight, anyway."

It was Peter's turn to be astonished. "You've got a boyfriend?"

"What's the matter? Did you think you were the only one interested? All I had to do was let him know I was available — "

"Who is he?" Peter demanded.

"No one you'd know," she said. Monica listened in wonder to her own lies, powerless to stop it. "He lives in Silver Spring."

"Oh. Well, have a good time," Peter said, recovering.

"You, too, Peter," Monica said. "And be sure to send my regards to Lisa."

Chapter **17**

This time, Monica thought, I should have listened to my horoscope. The day's prediction had forecasted great triumphs in the morning, but warned of strange encounters in the evening. She had had her triumph at WKND, and now she was seated across a table from a stranger, and feeling extremely wary.

Monica's hopes had been high when Carter Smith had picked her up about an hour earlier. He was easily six feet tall, and with his deep-set blue eyes, and a shock of perfectly sculpted dark brown curly hair, Carter easily could have passed as Tom Selleck's brother. During the ride to the restaurant in Carter's shining red Camaro, both Monica and Carter had chatted easily with Kim and Woody about school and Rose Hill. Now that they were seated at the American Cafe, Monica found herself with nothing to say, and Carter seemed to be in the same position.

Monica looked helplessly across the table at Kim. Carter was listening to Woody analyze a movie that was playing downtown. Carter was nodding his head occasionally, but he hadn't said a word about the movie, except that he had seen it. Monica wished they could have been sitting in a movie theater right then.

Kim coughed loudly. "Excuse me, boys. I've got to check out the facilities." She motioned for Monica to follow her.

"I'll be right back, too," Monica said, rising.

Monica hesitated when she saw that the ladies room housed one toilet with no stalls, but Kim pulled her in. "Look, you're too tense. Try to lighten up and have a good time."

"I know he's Woody's cousin, so he can't be all bad," Monica said, grimacing. "But it's a little bit like talking to a stone."

Kim rested a hand on her hip. "C'mon, Monica. You get a little shy at times, too. Try to get to know him. Ask him more questions about himself. Who knows? Maybe he's got a good sense of humor. Maybe he plays sports." Kim smiled. "He's gorgeous — that's one thing in his favor."

"Looks aren't everything." Monica sighed. "But I'll try my best."

"That's what we like to hear!" Kim punched Monica playfully on her shoulder. "By the way, I like that dress. Is it new?"

Monica had bought the dark blue, wide-skirted dress two weeks earlier, thinking of Peter's response as she turned in front of the mirrors at the department store. She had never worn it until this date. "Do you think Carter likes it?"

150

"There's only one way to find out." Kim opened the door to the ladies room, and Monica followed her. They both smiled and nodded to the wide-eyed woman who stood waiting to go into the bathroom.

Woody announced, "The waiter came by while you were gone. We took the liberty of ordering drinks. I asked for diet sodas for you."

"Thanks, Woody," Monica said. Turning to Carter she asked, "What are you drinking?"

"Milk," he answered. "I don't like soda. It's not good for you."

Monica decided not to ask if Carter had tried any of the new local DC Soda Company drinks. "Carter," she began. "That's quite an unusual first name. Is it an old family name?"

"It's been mine for seventeen years."

"Are there other Carters in the family?"

He looked down at the white china plate, lost in contemplation. Finally he answered, "No."

Woody piped up, "With a name like Smith, his parents wanted something unusual. It's like me. There are an awful lot of John and Richard Websters in this world, but not too many Woodys."

Kim nudged him gently. "Are you kidding? You're one of a kind."

The waiter returned to take their orders. Monica requested soft-shell crabs. Kim and Woody each ordered a shrimp dish. Carter ordered broiled sole. "No butter, please," he told the waiter. Turning to Monica he explained, "Too much cholesterol."

Monica thought Carter sounded a lot like

151

Sasha, who was a natural foods fanatic. "So you're into health foods?" she asked him.

"My whole family is, really." he said, smiling. "I've been designing a computer program to work out balanced diets for everyone according to age, life-style, and food preferences."

"Really? How do you do it?" Monica was relieved that she had stumbled onto one topic Carter was comfortable talking about.

"Do you understand BASIC?"

"BASIC what?"

"The programming language — BASIC."

Monica laughed. "No. My computer knowledge stopped when I got bored with Donkey Kong."

"Oh, if you really want to know about computers, games hardly scratch the surface. Take this diet program I wrote."

Monica tried to pay attention as Carter told her about statements, loops, and flowcharts. Her one serious exposure to computers had been a ninth-grade computer literacy course, in which she received her worst grade ever. She could only nod in what she hoped were the right places. When he finished, she decided to try another tack. "Do you play any sports?" she asked.

"I'm not on any teams," he said. "But I like to go skeet shooting."

"That's with guns, right?" she asked.

"Yes," he said, "but they're just clay targets. I'd never shoot at anything real. Have you ever shot?"

"I'm not very fond of guns," she admitted. "But I like to play tennis. Do you?"

Carter shook his head. "I don't think it's very challenging unless both players are really exceptional."

"Oh. Do you have any hobbies?"

"I'm a spelunker. You know, someone who likes to explore caves. This summer I'm going out to Colorado. I've heard there are some terrific caves out there. I can't wait to check them out."

"Oh, I bet that'll be exciting for you," she said. But visions of bats and bugs crowded her mind.

Monica felt she'd been given a reprieve when the dinners were served. She wanted to like Carter. He was handsome, he was friendly, and he even had good table manners. But she couldn't find anything they had in common.

As the foursome ate in silence, Monica's attention turned to the crowd in the restaurant. With each bite she took she looked around the room, hoping and dreading to see Peter with Lisa. She knew they were together, possibly nearby. But if Peter had taken Lisa out to eat, it hadn't been to the American Cafe.

Monica took a deep sip of her water. It felt as if the crab had stuck in her throat. Her entire body was tense with the pressure that came from the difficult evening. She drank the entire glass of water — the tension remained.

She might have drunk the entire Potomac River before Carter noticed. In the silence, his shyness had returned. He was staring at his plate, concentrating intently on his fish and baked potato. Monica wanted to make him relax. She

hated to think she was making him feel uncom-
fortable. Her frustration turned to sympathy.

"Did Woody tell you I work at our high school
radio station?" she asked.

"No."

"Does your high school have one?"

"No."

"What kind of music do you like?"

"All kinds, I guess."

"Any favorites?"

"Nothing in particular. Basic rock and roll."

"How come you don't play basketball, Carter?
You're tall enough."

"I tried out once, but the coach cut me. I
wasn't very good."

Carter continued to concentrate on his fish.
If there had been a moment in which to draw him
out, Monica had missed it. "So tell me about
your family," she said, groping for something to
talk about. "Do you have any brothers or sisters?"

"A brother and a sister. But they're both older.
Neither one has lived at home for about ten
years."

Monica sighed. She was out of questions,
Carter didn't feel inclined to ask her anything,
and Kim and Woody were too busy with their
private conversation to help her out.

It was going to be a very long night.

Chapter
18

Peter stared across the table in the Bistro Francais at Lisa, still not quite believing she was there. Lisa was just as beautiful as he had remembered. Her thick black hair was longer, and she wore it tied back in a French knot, emphasizing her slightly exotic eyes, and the smile that reminded him of a warm winter's fire.

"So, how does it feel to be back home?" he asked.

Lisa took a sip from the cut-crystal glass. "Colorado water tastes better." She smiled. "As for how it feels, well, it's too early to tell. I'm happy to see you again, and it's nice to take a break from my routine. Even if it's only for a weekend."

"Still worried about the national tryouts?"

"You bet. This new routine I'm doing is very difficult. It doesn't quite fit yet. That's part of the reason I came down here. I need some moral support from Mr. Helde." He was Lisa's long-time skating coach, and owner of the Capitol Skating Rink.

"I'm not surprised to hear that. What's so different about this new routine?"

"Oh, just some new moves." She took another sip of water. "That's not important, you are. How's WKND's favorite DJ?"

"Fine." He shrugged.

"And the station? You told me something about a new assistant. You've found someone who knows how to file records?"

"Yeah." Peter looked up at the stained glass light fixture overhead. He didn't want to talk about the station, it reminded him too much of Monica. He thought he had gotten her out of his system. He had tried acting strictly professional toward her all week, in an effort to forget his feelings for her. It hadn't worked, though her actions that afternoon made it clear he had managed to make her dislike him. He was ashamed that it upset him that she had found another boyfriend. It was selfish, but if he couldn't have her, he didn't want anyone else to have her, either.

Peter lowered his eyes toward Lisa. His speech to Monica was supposed to have made everything all right, but something was terribly wrong. He had been certain that when he saw Lisa again all his old feelings would come rushing back. But it was as if there was a glass wall separating them. He could see and hear the way things were, but he just couldn't feel it. Yet she seemed so delighted to be with him, he didn't have the heart to let her down, not with the nationals coming up. "So are you going to be performing your routine at the exhibition?"

"No. I'll be doing my old one."

"Why not the new one?"

"It'd be too difficult for me," Lisa said.

Peter could tell Lisa didn't feel like talking about it. He chalked it up to nerves. "Have you had a chance to talk to anyone else since you've been back?"

Peter felt as if he were conducting a WKND interview. He had been away from Lisa for so long, it was as if they had to introduce themselves to each other all over again. "I talked to Phoebe briefly," Lisa replied. "We made plans to meet on Sunday. She sounded like she was coming down with a cold. She wouldn't tell me anything about her visit with Griffin."

"Don't feel bad," Peter said. "She hasn't said a word to anybody. I guess that means it didn't go well."

"That's too bad. I really thought they had something special."

I thought we did, too, Peter said to himself, but Lisa's sad look made him wonder if she were thinking the same thing. She had lowered her head, and was concentrating completely on cutting her chicken into bite-sized bits. Then she looked up and said brightly, "Phoebe invited me to come over to her house tomorrow night, too. She said she was throwing a little party. Will you be going?"

"No," Peter said abruptly. He reached across the table for her hand. "It's not the type of thing I think you'd be interested in, Monica."

Peter wanted to bite his tongue. He drew his hand back as he felt his face redden. How could he have been so stupid?

Lisa lowered her eyes again. "Peter, I think we have to talk."

"I know," he said. "I'm really sorry — "

"No, let me talk," she said. "I've got a lot to say, and I think it'll be easier if I say it all in one piece. This new routine I have — it's with a boy. A few weeks ago, the coach pulled me into his office and told me point blank he didn't think I'd make the national team. He said it wasn't because I wasn't good, but because the competition is especially fierce this year. And if forced to choose, the judges are going to pick someone younger, someone who can skate through at least the next two Olympics. In skating, a seventeen-year-old is considered ancient. But he thought I stood a good chance if I switched to pairs skating, where the skaters are usually older. He matched me with a guy named Dallas — from El Paso, of all places. He's very sweet and, well, I don't know how to say this, but I want to go out with him. I haven't yet, because I still care very deeply about you, and the promise I made. But, Peter, I don't know when I'll be back in Rose Hill, and it's not fair to make you wait for me, either. Do you know what I mean?" She had been speaking in a torrent, and Peter sat silently across from her, waiting for her to finish. She finally looked up at him, and the expression on his face clearly surprised her. "Peter, you're smiling!"

He reached for her hand. "I hope you understand what I'm going to say to you. You've just made me a very happy guy. See, I've been thinking the same thing. There's a girl here in Rose Hill I care a lot about. I haven't really dated her because of what you meant to me. But I'd like to. It's not that I don't care about you anymore — I think I always will, in a way. But it seems impossible to go on like this, not knowing when we might be together next."

"I think you're right." Lisa squeezed his hand tighter. "You know what that makes us, Lacey?"

"What?"

"Good friends." She smiled. "I'm glad it's working out this way. I really cherish your friendship, and I'd feel just awful if I had to lose that. I can't tell you how much it meant to me when I got to Colorado. I was scared, and lonely, on my own for the first time in my life. Knowing there was someone back here who was waiting for me helped me get through those first few weeks."

Peter felt an enormous relief. "I'm glad you were able to find someone to care about out there. So he's a pretty good skater, huh?"

Lisa giggled. "He'd better be, if he's going to be my partner." Then she took a sip of water and nodded. "He was a junior champion in Texas."

"I didn't know they had rinks in Texas."

"They're all over the country, silly."

"I'd still like to watch you skate tomorrow."

159

"I'd still love to have you there. You can even bring your new girl friend."

He eyed her curiously. "You wouldn't mind?"

"Well, maybe a little," she admitted. "But I wouldn't want to stop you from taking her if you wanted to."

"Thanks, but I don't think I'll be taking you up on the offer. See, I'm not sure she still wants me. She's out with another guy tonight."

"That doesn't necessarily mean anything. You're out with another girl," Lisa pointed out. "What's she like? She must be special to get you worked up like this."

"She is." Even though Peter was looking right at Lisa, he pictured Monica as clearly as if she was sitting there instead. He saw her as she was that afternoon, with his oversized headphones covering her ears, a smile as wide as the Beltway as she spoke into the microphone. At the time he had had to fight himself not to wrap her in his arms and tell her how proud he was of her, and how beautiful she looked to him.

"Earth to Peter. Earth to Peter." Lisa's waving arms brought him back to the present. "I seemed to have lost you there."

He smiled sheepishly. "Her name's Monica. She works with me at WKND. She even did her own show this afternoon."

Lisa nearly choked on her chicken. "Now I've heard everything. You gave up your air time voluntarily? Or did she put a gun to your head?"

Peter laughed. "Monica's not like that at all. She really wants to be a DJ — as much as I do, if that's possible. She's sharp, too, and she challenges me, which helps make me a better DJ."

"So it's been a strictly professional relationship."

"Not exactly," he said slyly. "She's got some other good points besides a good voice."

"I hope so," Lisa said. "I really hope you can work things out with her."

"Just hope her date was a dog," he said. He looked down at his veal, and realized that he was ravenously hungry.

At Peter walked Lisa up the brick path to her house, he was both content and sad. He was glad he and Lisa were parting as friends, but the transition was having its awkward moments. It felt a little strange, to be so close and comfortable with her, and yet to be giving her up. He held her hand firmly in his, well aware it would be the last time he would do so.

"I had a really good time with you, Lisa," he told her, as they reached the door.

Lisa looked up at him with wide-open eyes. Peter thought they looked moist. "I had a good time, too, Peter. I'm sorry about the way it's worked out. I never thought we'd be standing here like this, saying good-bye."

"This wasn't the script I wrote, either. But you have to admit it's what we both want. I'm glad it's ending this way, and not with us screaming 'I hate you' at each other."

"I could never hate you, Peter," she whispered.

"Lisa, you'll always be special to me." Peter

gently cupped his hands on Lisa's cheeks and kissed her. Immediately, she clasped his neck and held him tightly, until the sound of someone on the other side of the door caused them to move apart.

Chapter
19

"It was nice of you to throw this party for me, Phoebe." Monica was pouring herself a soda. She practically had to shout out the words. Phoebe had turned the stereo up to the limit.

"My pleasure," Phoebe answered, trying to be as sociable as she could. She was dressed in black: black jeans, black safari shirt tied with a sash, and huge, black-plastic hoop earrings. Chris had told her she looked like a living pack of licorice. Phoebe wore the outfit because she wanted something to match her mood.

Monica pointed to the stereo. Ted was thumbing through Phoebe's record collection for something to play. "I'm surprised you didn't ask me to be DJ tonight."

"You're the guest of honor. You're supposed to have fun," Phoebe said. "I asked Peter to come — he usually volunteers to pick out the records at my parties — but he turned me down.

I thought he would want to be here. After all, he's the one who put you on the air and all."

"I'm sure he's got better things to do," Monica said. She could hear the hollow ring of her voice, and wondered if Phoebe did, too. But she was glad she didn't have to face Peter. "His girl friend Lisa is in town this weekend."

Phoebe nodded. "She's also a good friend of mine. I saw her exhibition this afternoon. Did Peter tell you about her? I invited her to come, but she said no, too." Phoebe smiled wistfully. "I guess the two of them would rather be alone."

Monica picked up her glass and turned. "I see Kim over there. Excuse me, Phoebe." Quickly, she walked to the front door and greeted Kim and Woody as they arrived.

Phoebe munched on a potato chip and wondered why Monica seemed to be upset. It was turning out to be a very strange weekend. Lisa had virtually bubbled about life in Colorado, but was strangely vague about her date with Peter the night before, telling her to ask Peter. But Peter hadn't wanted to talk with her, either. And now, Monica Ford also flinched at the subject.

At least this situation helped Phoebe get her mind off Griffin. Since she had returned from New York she had grown progressively more depressed, thinking about everything she had done wrong during the trip. She was convinced Mrs. Webster was just being kind by telling her Griffin was going to call. The weekend was half over, and she hadn't heard a word from him. With each passing hour, the likelihood grew greater that she never would again.

Chris sidled up next to her and gave her a playful nudge. "So how come Kennedy High's Civil War expert is pouting? I heard you blew 'em away in Novato's class yesterday," she said.

"You didn't hear it from him," Phoebe answered with a snort. "He thought I pulled a fast one on him, getting Howard to do my report on Wednesday. He told me after class that I'd given an A-plus presentation, but because I'd done the switch he was knocking it down to a B."

"That's not fair!" Chris exclaimed.

Phoebe shrugged. "It was a no-win situation."

Chris was incensed. "I'm going to go to him on Monday and give him a piece of my mind."

Phoebe held up a hand. "Don't waste your time. I'm just glad the whole thing's over."

Chris put down her soda and grabbed Phoebe by the arms. "Look, I don't know what happened between you and Griffin, but you're not going to feel better about it until you tell someone." She laughed. "That's what you always tell me."

Phoebe turned her head. "Maybe I want to feel miserable."

Chris cocked her head, tilting it so it almost rested on her own shoulder. "This isn't the Phoebe Hall I know. Talk to me. Did Griffin hurt you?"

Phoebe raced out of the room, up the stairs to her bedroom. She flung herself on her bed, burying her head between her two pillows. Chris followed her up the stairs, and closed the door behind her. She leaned against the door, folding her arms like a sentry. "You're not leaving this

165

room till you tell me what happened," she said. "I'll wait forever."

Phoebe raised her head. "What if you get hungry?" She plopped back between the pillows.

Chris moved closer to the bed. She knelt on her long legs so she was eye level with the pillows. "Knowing you, you'll get hungry first."

Phoebe peeked out again. "Thirsty?"

"There's water in your bathroom." Chris smiled. "C'mon, Phoebe, it's me, Chris. You can talk with me. I won't let anything out of this room."

Slowly Phoebe lifted her head. Through her teary eyes, Chris was a blur of blond hair mixed with the red wool from her sweater. She wiped her eyes with her shirt sleeve. "I don't know, Chris. I haven't felt like myself today." She used her other sleeve to wipe away a fresh set of tears.

"Let it out, Phoebe. You'll feel better."

Phoebe heaved a deep sigh. "I feel like the world's biggest fool. Chris, did you ever feel like you had something slip through your fingers? That's how I feel now." Phoebe lifted herself up, propping the pillows behind her back. "I couldn't leave well enough alone. I had it in my head that Griffin wouldn't be satisfied with good old me; he would want a real New York City girl. What he ended up with was a phony. I did a lot of stupid things in New York that I don't want to talk about, but the worst thing I did was not act like myself. I picked a fight with Griffin over the dumbest thing. It would serve me right if he never wanted to see me again."

166

Chris sat down on the bed. "Did he tell you that?"

"He didn't have to."

"Well, how did you leave things?"

"I'd left my clothes in his apartment — "

"You what?"

"I know what that dirty mind of yours is thinking," Phoebe smirked. "It was totally innocent. I got soaked in a rainstorm. Anyway, Griffin returned them to my hotel room. I wasn't there, but he told Mrs. Webster he'd call this weekend. But it's already Saturday night, and I haven't heard a word. I probably never will."

"Phoebe Hall, you're right. You're a class-A jerk. I've never seen anyone get so worked up over nothing. He said he'd call."

"Why haven't I heard from him, then?"

"He said this weekend, but he didn't say when. There's still half a weekend left. I'll bet my presidency he'll call." She rose from the bed and held out her hand. "Come on, there's a roomful of people eating up your food downstairs. You ought to be there with them."

Phoebe took her friend's hand. "Okay." She rolled up the sleeves of her safari shirt to hide the wet tearstains. "Austin, remind me not to invite you the next time I throw a pity party."

Sasha met them at the foot of the stairs. "Hey, where have you two been hiding? We're about to toast Monica!"

Phoebe felt a little chagrined. It wasn't right to throw a party and not be around for the celebration. She trotted over to the table and poured herself a soda. As Monica walked over, Phoebe rapped her hand on the tabletop. "Attention, everyone!" Gradually the room quieted down, and she continued, "As you know, this isn't just a typical Saturday night get-together. We're here to celebrate the debut performance of WKND's latest star — Monica Ford."

As Woody led an impromptu cheer, Monica felt herself turning as red as Chris's sweater. She wasn't used to this much attention. It was like trying on brand-new shoes — they were the right size, perhaps, but still not completely comfortable.

Phoebe continued her toast. "Congratulations, Monica. I hope you continue to rock Kennedy High for a long time to come." She lifted her glass and downed the soda in one long gulp.

The crowd surrounded Monica as they watched her drink to her own toast. Sasha said, "I guess we won't be seeing much of you around the paper anymore."

"Probably not. WKND can be time-consuming."

Ted leaned toward her. "I like you, Monica, and you seem to really be into this radio stuff. So let me give you some advice. Peter's not around, so I feel free to tell you this. Romance and radio don't mix."

"Oh, Ted," Chris scoffed, "Monica's not like that. She's got brains."

"So does Janie Barstow, and that didn't stop her from getting a crush on Lacey," he explained. Turning back to Monica he added, "Janie totally misread Peter's professional interest. When he found out that she had a crush on him, and she found out that he liked someone else, that little studio got too small for both of them."

"Well, Monica doesn't have to worry about it. She knows Peter's already taken," Phoebe said.

If only they knew the real story, Monica thought. She wanted this conversation to end. It was hitting way too close to home. Maybe Peter had been playing with her affections, the way he had with Janie's? She forced herself to speak. "Peter is just my co-worker, nothing more. Last night I met a guy who's eons apart from Peter. I had a great time with him."

Kim and Woody turned to stare at her. Monica avoided their looks. Ten minutes earlier she had called Carter Smith the black hole of Silver Spring.

"Really? What's he like?" Phoebe asked.

"He's so unique it's hard to put it into words. Mostly he's the strong, silent type." With the emphasis on silent, she wanted to add. "And very deep. So deep, I'm sure I only scratched the surface with him." She sighed. "I just hope he feels the same way about me."

"But he does," Woody said. "He had a great time with you. I know he'd love to go out with you again."

"So when are you going to see him again?" Phoebe asked.

What am I getting myself into? Monica wondered.

* * *

169

"Pheebee!" The din of the room was shattered by Shawn's piercing cry from the second floor. "Telephone for Pheebee!"

Phoebe stiffened. Chris looked at her and smiled knowingly. But Phoebe was so nervous she could hardly walk to the phone. There was only one person it could be, only one person she wanted it to be. But she dreaded hearing what he had to say.

She picked up the phone. "Hello?"

"Phoebe, glad to catch you in." The boy on the other end sounded exuberant, but nothing like Griffin.

"Who is this?"

"Howard. Howard Walker. This is the first chance I've had to thank you for saving my life in Novato's class. You wrote a great report. He gave me a B."

"Gee, Howard, that's great," Phoebe said numbly. She wondered how to get him off the phone.

"I couldn't have done it without you. Hey, what's a gorgeous girl like you doing home on a Saturday night?" When she didn't answer right away, he added, "It sounds like you've got a party going on."

The last thing Phoebe wanted was an evening with her candidate for geek of the week. "Oh, that's my brother," she babbled. "He's watching a party movie on the video. He likes the sound turned up loud."

"Oh," he said. "Well, maybe I'll call you sometime."

"Good-night, Howard." Phoebe put down the receiver before he could answer.

She ran to her room and slammed the door closed. She didn't care what Chris had told her before — this was her house, and if she wanted to spend the rest of the night in her room, she would. The party would be fine without her.

She had been so sure the phone call was from Griffin. Now she was more depressed than before. She couldn't stop being a fool when it came to him. First the episodes in New York, now her waiting around for him to call.

She picked up a copy of *Seventeen* and began flipping the pages. Her eye caught an ad that featured an ice skater. It made her think of Lisa, and how beautiful she had looked during her exhibition that afternoon. Lisa had sacrificed a lot to be a skater, so much so, that she had often told Phoebe how she envied her ability to have a social life. Now Phoebe wondered if Lisa hadn't been the wiser of the two. By dedicating herself to her skating, she hadn't had time to deal with the heartbreak of relationships.

Phoebe heard the phone ring again. Shawn can get it, she told herself. The next thing she heard was his bellowing "Pheebee!" into the hall.

Reluctantly she rose from her bed. "Howard, I don't want to talk to you," she hissed under her breath. But her heart was racing again, and she knew that as long as the phone kept ringing, she would keep hoping to hear Griffin's voice on the other end of the line.

Chapter 20

Peter twisted the dial of his car radio, searching for a station with decent music. The D.C. station he usually listened to the most had pulled a mean trick on him, devoting the evening to the top ten heavy metal bands of all time. Another station was playing non-stop commercials.

He tuned in another station in time to hear the DJ say, "And this song goes out to a very special couple, Dean and Barbara, who've pledged their eternal love to each other. Ah, isn't that a dedication to end all dedications. . . ."

"No," Peter answered, turning off the radio. Disgusted, he popped a tape into the cassette player. Moments later his four state-of-the-art speakers were blaring out, *"Born in the U.S.A. . . . Born in the U.S.A. . . ."*

Peter rested his fingers on the steering wheel and smiled for the first time all day. He knew he could count on the Boss to make things all right.

It had been a miserable day. That morning, while helping his dad with the yard work, he gashed his shin. For a while it was bleeding so badly he thought he would have to get some stitches. He didn't, but it still felt terribly sore.

The little accident put him behind schedule, and he walked into Lisa's exhibition after she had begun. He was surprised at the turnout — she had a lot more fans than he'd realized. There were even several photographers there. Rose Hill had only one paper, so he wondered where the others were from. There was one from the *Washington Post*, another from the training camp in Colorado. He had shaken his head. The night before he thought he had lost her to just another skater. At the rink, he began to see he had lost her to the rest of the world.

He should have been sitting at rinkside, next to the Changs, and Phoebe and Sasha, but there was no more room left for him. So, Peter had taken one of the few remaining seats near the top of the bleachers.

Lisa was moving around the rink like a miniature rocket. She did jumps and spins with a precision that brought oohs and aahs from the audience. She had a confidence and command of herself that Peter had never seen, the results of the months of intense training in the Rockies. He was immensely proud of her, but in a detached way, as if the black-and-white costumed sprite on the ice were a vision from the past. Even though he didn't want her, it still unnerved him to realize she didn't belong to him anymore. She didn't need him to cheer her on with every move, to hold his breath in the anxious moments between the start of a jump and the time she landed in a graceful spin. He wouldn't be there, as he had so often dreamed, to hand her a dozen red roses as she left the ice in the Olympic arena.

Peter had left before Lisa completed her show. He had felt superfluous, as unneeded and unwanted as the stupid subscription cards that came with every issue of *Rolling Stone*. He would always have warm feelings about Lisa, but he would have felt awkward waiting for her. He had looked at the waiting row of male skaters near the ice, and briefly wondered if one of them might be Lisa's new partner. Then he'd made his way toward the door.

Peter sang along with Bruce Springsteen. It wasn't the way he wanted to spend Saturday night, but he was too restless to do anything but drive around Rose Hill.

He wound up in front of Phoebe's house. The front rooms were lit up, and he could hear the faint sounds of music. He wanted to go inside. All his friends were there, including the one person he wanted to see most of all — Monica.

Peter sat through three Springsteen songs, trying to get up the nerve to leave his car. This is weird, this is really weird, he kept telling himself. He'd never been shy about telling a girl what was on his mind.

But as he had learned already, Monica was different from other girls. She had made it clear Friday that she did not intend to wait for him to change his mind about Lisa. He shouldn't have been surprised that she already had a boyfriend. She was pretty, and intelligent, and funny. And as the new voice on WKND, she'd probably gained half the male population at school as secret admirers. He had probably missed his one chance at Monica Ford.

At least, he thought, he no longer had anything to lose by telling her how he felt. And he was definitely willing to wait for her. Monday morning, he decided, he would let her know.

"Phoebe, is that you? What's going on? It sounds as if you're having a party."

"Griffin?" After her earlier letdown, Phoebe could hardly believe it was really him. A little bit of her faith in humanity — and Griffin — was restored.

"Yeah, it's me. I told Mrs. Webster I'd call you. Didn't she give you the message?"

"Yes," Phoebe said dully. She still dreaded what he had to say.

"You don't sound right, Phoebe. Are you still mad at me?"

"I was never mad at you," she blurted.

She could hear his breath of relief. "Boy, you had me worried there for a while."

"But I'm sorry about the way I ran out on you," she added.

"Well, don't be." He said it with such conviction that Phoebe got scared, but only momentarily. He continued on. "You did me a tremendous favor."

"What are you talking about?"

"Maybe I ought to explain everything in person." His voice was as buoyant as ever. It gave Phoebe reason to hope he still cared.

"Griffin, are you planning on coming down to Rose Hill?"

"No, I'm already here. I'm calling from my house."

"Griffin Neill, get over here right this minute!" Phoebe cried. "Why didn't you tell me sooner?"

"I love the drama," he said. "Be over in ten minutes." He blew a kiss into the phone. "And I love you, too."

Phoebe put down the kitchen extension, ran past her guests to her room, and tore off her shirt. She had to change. Black would definitely no longer do. She had no time to think, so she grabbed the first thing out of her closet, her blue Cub Scout shirt. She smiled. It was a good omen; it was the shirt she wore the day she met Griffin. She ran a comb through her hair, brushed another layer of peach blush on her cheeks, and walked downstairs just as the doorbell rang.

Griffin was holding a bunch of wildflowers in his hand. He peered inside. "Hey, you *are* having a party."

Phoebe pulled him inside. "For my friend, Monica. She did her first WKND radio show yesterday. Now tell me what you're doing here."

"Giving you these." He handed her the flowers.

"They're nice," she said, sniffing them. She walked toward the kitchen. "Where'd you get them?"

"A garden down the block."

Phoebe thought they looked familiar. "Not

Mrs. Cormier's!" She started to laugh. "You're crazy, Neill." She bopped him over the head with the bunch.

"It takes one to know one." He winked. "That was some disappearing act you pulled the other day."

Phoebe put the flowers on the counter. "I was a real idiot. I thought the more sophisticated I acted, the better I'd fit in. I should have just been myself. Will you ever forgive me?"

"I was never upset with you. I couldn't blame you for being upset about my apartment, or my criticism of your singing. I thought you were acting a little strange the rest of the time, but it was nothing that made me mad."

"Don't remind me. But I felt awful about running out the way I did. I went back to your apartment, but you'd already left for the theater. Then I went backstage after the show and you'd already gone."

"You mean you saw the play?"

"Didn't you see me in the audience?"

"No, I can't see anyone from the stage." Griffin stared at her, his blue-gray eyes flashing. "From the way you ran out, I didn't think you would come to the show. I thought you had gone back to the hotel. I waited for you there for an hour, until Mrs. Webster showed up."

She shook her head. "I was so upset you left the theater, I went out to a movie. Then I got mad at myself when I heard I missed you."

"Don't be. It was the best thing you could have done."

"That's what you said on the telephone. What happened?"

Griffin leaned against the kitchen counter. "I had a long talk with Mrs. Webster. She told me the Arena Theater was having tryouts for next season, and invited me to come down to audition. So that's what I did — today."

"Why didn't you tell me?"

"I was pretty nervous. I thought if you knew, you'd want to come to the audition. I asked her not to tell you, either."

"So did you make it?"

"I don't know yet. I don't know if I'm ready to give up on New York, either. Though there is one huge benefit of getting to act at the Arena."

"Sure. It's the biggest place you could play around here without already being a famous actor."

"Yes, there's that," he said. "But the biggest benefit would be being able to see you more often."

"Oh, Griffin." Phoebe felt herself beginning to cry. She had had so little faith in Griffin's love, she had imagined he would dump her over one bad day. She never should have doubted him.

"Those better be tears of joy. I'd hate to think I came here for nothing."

"How's this for proof?" Phoebe threw herself against him and held him so tightly, her arms hurt. Her tears were leaving blotches on his shirt. "When will you know?"

"They're having auditions all week. They'll be making their final selections by next weekend."

"How long will you be here?"

"I'm leaving first thing in the morning."

Phoebe pushed herself away. "So soon?"

He looked out through the picture window that faced the patio. "I still have the show in New York. I can't go burning bridges behind me, until I know where I'm going."

"I'll be here, waiting — no matter what happens," she said. "In the meantime, we have the rest of tonight." She leaned her head in the direction of the music. "I've already got a celebration going on." Taking his arm, she led him back into the party.

Chapter
21

Monica could hear the music coming out of the WKND studio at the far end of the hall. She looked at her watch. It wasn't quite twelve o'clock and Peter insisted on beginning his show at exactly noon. She wondered what he was doing.

He was combing his hair to the beat of the Front Lines, she saw as she looked into the studio. He faced the mirror on the side wall of the studio, running his red plastic comb along the side of his head, bobbing up and down in time with the music. He was whistling, too. No one deserves to be that happy, Monica thought, especially when she was feeling so miserable.

Monica took a few deep breaths before passing through the station door. Deep breathing was supposed to be relaxing, but all this did was make her lightheaded. She looked up at the ceiling, and counted the holes in the acoustical tile. If she stared at Peter she would crumble.

When she had regained her control, Monica marched ahead through the studio door, catching Peter as he peered into the mirror. He hastily stuffed the comb in the back pocket of his drawstring pants. "Uh, hi there, music fans," he greeted her in his best DJ voice.

Monica gasped. Peter looked even more handsome than usual. The pants were new, and he'd rolled up the sleeves of his T-shirt to reveal muscular arms. His skin was slightly golden, with a late spring tan.

Monica shook her head, trying to concentrate on her purpose in coming to the station. She didn't care how Peter looked, she told herself. His appearance, and his joyful mood, had to have been a residual from his weekend with Lisa. He was flaunting it in front of Monica, with his whistling and playing pre-show music.

Peter's thoughtless behavior strengthened Monica's resolve. "Peter," she began. Her voice was hesitant, but she plunged on anyway. "I can't work here anymore."

Peter was clearly stunned. He slumped back against the edge of the control board. Not a trace remained of his glee or playfulness. "You mean today?"

"No. Forever." She dug into her oversized brown shoulder bag, and handed him some manuals. "I'm returning these to you. I won't be needing them now."

Peter did not respond. He let the manuals drop

to the floor. "Monica, could we talk about this? I think — "

"No, Peter, I've done a lot of thinking. You know, it's been a big joke for me to try to work here ever since that evening we spent together."

"Monica, it doesn't have to be."

"Peter, it can't be any other way. I've thought a lot about it all weekend. I really care about you, and it's killing me to be so close to you and not be able to do anything about it."

"But I thought you cared about the station."

"I do, but the pressure is too much for me. Don't worry, I'm not abandoning my goals. I'm grateful you gave me the chance to do the show the other day. Now that I know I can do it, I'll pick it up again in college." She started to turn. "I'd better go, before I act like a real dope."

Peter looked at Monica, then at the clock. It was five seconds to twelve. "Wait right there," he cautioned her. Then he grabbed the mike and turned on the transmitter. "Hello there, Kennedy High music lovers. This is Peter Lacey welcoming you to the Monday show on WKND. To start things off here's an old favorite by Madonna, 'Crazy for You.' This one goes out from a guy who's trying to convince a very special girl that he cares."

As he turned back to Monica, he eyed the record closet. He lowered his eyes and pleaded with her. "Before you go, could you do me one last favor?"

"Peter, I — "

Peter nodded furiously. "I know I hurt you, Monica. I'm sorry, and I'm not going to press the issue any further. But I need some records right away. Will you please pick them out for me? Then I promise, I'll let you go."

Monica realized with a shock that Peter's only dismay came from losing his best assistant ever. She clenched her fists at her sides and fought the impulse to shout at him. She had come into WKND as a professional, and she would depart as one. Five minutes more, and she would be rid of Peter Lacey forever. "Certainly, Peter," she said, forcing a smile.

Numbly Monica walked to the closet, past the door that had been propped open ever since the day the lock had broken. She laughed; that day was ancient history. She had been foolish and naive then, thinking she was different from Janie Barstow, or other girls Peter might have hurt. It was an experience that left her sadder, but much wiser.

Monica stood facing the shelves of records, then realized with a start that Peter hadn't given her a list. She turned around to ask him what albums he wanted and found herself nose-to-chest with him. He had followed her into the closet. In that same instant that Monica turned, the door closed behind them with a thud.

Peter's hands grasped Monica's shoulders. She began to tremble. "Hey, don't worry," he said softly. "I'm not going to hurt you."

"No more than you have already?"

"Please listen to me," he pleaded.

She looked around the tiny space. "You've left me no choice."

183

"Lisa and I broke up this weekend."

Monica looked at him through disbelieving eyes.

"I told her all about you," Peter continued. "She wished me good luck with you. We both realized we were keeping our relationship alive on the basis of a promise that no longer had anything to do with love."

"Really?" Monica still wasn't ready to believe him.

Peter nodded. "As soon as I saw her, I knew that whatever we once had was just a memory now. I wanted to tell you sooner, but I was afraid."

"Of what?" she asked.

"That you might think I was choosing you, just because I couldn't have Lisa anymore. But it's not that way at all. It's like I told you that night at your house — I was holding on to her for sentimental reasons. You and I have shared more in the past couple of weeks at the station than I've had with Lisa in months."

Monica looked up into Peter's face, and saw in an instant how much he really cared about her. She had never felt so happy.

"I take back my resignation," Monica said with a broad smile.

Peter unsuccessfully fought the grin that took over his face.

"I accept, but on one condition."

"What's that?"

"That you let me take you out tonight."

"Accepted," she said.

"It's not final till we seal it with a kiss." He grabbed her by the waist and kissed her.

As Monica leaned against Peter's warm cotton shirt, she realized that the outfit, the hair combing, and the whistling had been for her. Peter had wanted to be with her as much as she wanted to be with him.

Monica wanted to rest against Peter's chest forever, but was distracted by a strange sound. "What's that?" she asked him, looking around.

Peter recognized the *da-thump, da-thump, da-thump* of the needle hitting the end of the record. "My show!" he exclaimed. Abruptly pulling away from Monica, he stepped toward the door and turned the handle. It wouldn't budge. "We're locked in."

Monica, who was leaning against the shelves that held the records, slid to the floor and extended a hand. "Come on down, and have a seat. Someone's going to notice you're off the air and check it out. In the meantime, let's make the most of it."

"This is the first time in two years I've missed a show," Peter said.

"I'm sorry," Monica apologized.

"Don't be," Peter said, as he slid down the wall next to her. "If I had to choose between the show and you, I'd miss it every day."

COUPLES

Coming Soon...
Couples #9
BROKEN HEARTS

Suddenly Phoebe was aware tears were running down her cheeks. She didn't bother to wipe them away. She knew she looked awful when she cried, but she didn't care. All she cared about was that the guy she loved and trusted had let her down.

"Wait a minute!" Griffin exclaimed. "I don't believe this. You mean you thought I didn't call you because I was with Sarah? That's the girl who's the lead in *West Side Story*. She's an actress. I just met her. She gave the whole pile of us a ride back — "

"Back?" Phoebe rubbed her face against her shirt sleeve. "Back from where?" she asked suspiciously.

"Oh, Phoebe!" Griffin took her in his arms. She didn't hug him back. "Phoebe, I love you. Don't you believe that? We were stuck there all night; the whole cast was — at Bob Jacob's house. The reading went on past midnight. A couple of us didn't have cars, so Sarah offered to drive us back on her way into Georgetown."

Phoebe searched Griffin's blue eyes a second. She could tell he wasn't lying. "Oh, Griffin, I'm sorry. I just didn't know what to think. I mean — " She twisted and untwisted the towel in her hands. She looked down at the limp piece of striped cotton and giggled slightly as she tossed it on the counter. "Look at me. I'm such a mess." With one hand she tentatively touched Griffin's arm. "I just got worried, that's all. And I so wanted to know how you did."

"As I said the other night, you're the one who gets dramatic." Griffin smiled and bent to kiss her. A few seconds later he pulled her out the back door, and they sat down together on the concrete steps. Although it was a warm May day, the concrete was still cold and damp against Phoebe's bare thighs. Doing all her hand wash at once had reduced her to wearing a pair of baggy Bermuda shorts and her short-sleeved Boy Scout shirt.

Griffin cleared his throat and toyed with Phoebe's green plastic earrings as he spoke. "I guess I'm not used to being worried about, Pheeb. It's flattering but — please try not to worry about me. Not that way. The whole time in New York there was no other girl but you."

"I know that, Griffin," Phoebe said softly.